DOCTOR WHO

DECIDE YOUR DESTINY

EMPIRE OF THE WOLF

BBC CHILDREN'S BOOKS
Published by the Penguin Group
Penguin Books Ltd, 80 Strand, London, WC2R 0RL, England
Penguin Group (USA) Inc., 375 Hudson Street, New York 10014, USA
Penguin Books (Australia) Ltd, 250 Camberwell Road, Camberwell, Victoria 3124, Australia
(A division of Pearson Australia Group Pty Ltd)
Canada, India, New Zealand, South Africa
Published by BBC Children's Books, 2010
Text and design © Children's Character Books, 2010
Written by Neil Corry
001 – 10 9 8 7 6 5 4 3 2 1
BBC logo © BBC 1996. Doctor Who logo © BBC 2009. TARDIS image © BBC 1963.
Licensed by BBC Worldwide Limited.
BBC, DOCTOR WHO (word marks, logos and devices), and TARDIS are trademarks of the
British Broadcasting Corporation and are used under licence.
ISBN: 978-1-40590-715-6
Printed in Great Britain by Clays Ltd, St Ives plc

How To Use Your Decide Your Destiny Book

Follow the instructions below before reading this book.

1. Go to: www.doctorwhochildrensbooks.co.uk/decideyourdestiny

2. Click 'Begin' to launch the book selection screen.

3. After selecting your book, the scene selection menu will appear.

4. Start reading the story on page 1 of this book and follow the instructions at the end of each section.

5. When you make a decision that takes you online, select the correct box and enter the corresponding code word as prompted.

6. After watching the scene or completing your online activity, return to the scene selection screen and continue your story.

Now turn the page and begin your adventure!

You are cycling home from school one November afternoon. You live in a small town to the west of Aberdeen, not far from Balmoral Castle, the Queen's summer residence. It gets dark early in Scotland in November and you're grateful for the full moon rising in the early evening sky. It helps you see your way home. There aren't many streetlamps around. Your breath is like fog as you race along the road. There's no one about and, although you can hear what sounds like a motorbike in the distance, it feels like you could be the only person in the world. It's a cold evening and all you want to do is get home and get warm again.

Up ahead you see a large figure lumber into the road. It casts a strange silhouette in the moonlight. Some instinct kicks in and you know that something about the figure is very wrong. But what do you do?

If you trust your instincts and race away, go to 17.

If you decide to fight your instincts and investigate, go to 44.

As the helicopter descends you see the ruins up close. You realise that maybe this wasn't the best idea after all. The noise from the aircraft has attracted curious werewolves to step outside the dilapidated building. In the strange light shining from the abandoned monastery, you see silhouettes of the beasts on four legs, some on their hind legs, their eyes glinting – and they all seem to be looking right at you!

The monsters keep away from the helicopter – but that situation won't last long. As soon as you land you'll be sitting ducks, ready to be torn apart by the supernatural menaces.

'Should we be doing this, Doctor?' you ask nervously and loudly as the aircraft comes to land.

'It's too late for a change of plan,' he calls back. 'I can't guess how much time we've got left before...' he trails off.

'Before what?' shouts Amy over the din of the helicopter.

'I can't be sure! But I have the oddest feeling that when the moon is as its highest we'll find out and it'll be too late!'

While the pilot lands, the other soldier – Eric something-or-other – fires a machine gun at the wolf creatures. They roar in fury but still stay back.

Amy and then the Doctor carefully jump out of the machine, their hair whipping their faces, their clothes blowing madly in the wind. The Doctor expects you to follow and holds out a hand to help you down.

You jump and are shocked when the helicopter takes off. The pilot's left you defenceless!

This is truly terrifying and you're suddenly unsure of yourself. Surely it'd be madness to face who knows how many werewolves like this? Should you, in fact, be doing this?

If you think yes, you have to help in any way you can, go to 49.

If you think no, but you're going to help anyway, go to 53.

You, the Doctor and Amy walk through crumbling corridors, stepping over debris and puddles of acrid water towards the light's source. You reach what you think was once a large room. It no longer has a roof, one wall has collapsed and you see that there's more outside than inside.

But that doesn't shock you. Nor does the column of light reaching endlessly into the sky, filling the place with so much radiance that it bleaches the colour from everything. The beam itself is fascinating, with swirling strands rising through the beam towards the heavens. Its power seems immense.

You, Amy and the Doctor stand absolutely still. Gathered around the light, almost as if praying to it, are dozens of werewolves, their forelegs outstretched, their hind legs tucked under their bodies, and their heads lying on the ground. Seeing how still they are chills you to the core. To see so many of them acting as if they're waiting for something to happen is terrifying – how much worse can it be?

The Doctor points to the sky and whispers, 'Look at the moon, through the clouds, it's about to pass through the light's path. We don't have time to be careful.'

Gingerly but quickly, the Doctor steps over the dormant monsters towards the light. At its base is a weird-looking stone platform with a pile of earth around it.

'This must have arrived with the haemovariform when it crashed all those years ago,' he says. 'Has it been growing here ever since, just as the haemovariform did?'

You're not sure what the Doctor's talking about.

If you're happy to stay where you are, away from the werewolves, go to 28.

If you want to take a closer look at the peculiar stone, go to 38.

The Doctor laughs after you suggest the police, then says that what's happening is rather too specialised for the police.

'And,' he adds, 'I've had hundreds of years of practise at this sort of thing. They'd only get in the way. So it looks like it's just us three. Are you ready?'

You don't get time to reply — and you're not sure what your reply would be! He revs the motorbike's engine and you, Amy and the Doctor are away!

The roads are deserted — it's as if everyone knows something terrible is coming and has decided to stay home. You check your watch. It's not even five o'clock. In the distance you see a strange light from a building in the middle of a field.

'That's the old monastery,' you tell the Doctor. 'It's supposed to be just ruins.'

The Doctor slows and stops the bike. He pulls out a wand-like device from his pocket and tells you and Amy to be careful. The 'sonic screwdriver' is picking up alien technology.

'Alien?' you ask.

'Yes, stuff not of this world that doesn't belong here,' says the Doctor. 'It's most likely something to do with the werewolves. I mean, I like coincidences, but I don't trust them.'

'Let's get on with it, then,' says Amy, stepping out of the sidecar.

The rest of your journey is on foot, as you cross a boggy field towards the ruins. You make out an entrance on the left and one straight on. The weird light is suddenly replaced by a phenomenal column of light shooting into the sky. It seems to go on forever and you can't see the end of it. What's causing it? You want to know but dread finding out.

The Doctor passes you an old-fashioned perfume bottle. 'You might need this. I don't think we've much time.'

Suddenly there's a howl from behind you. You all turn to see three werewolves standing on their hind legs with the moon high behind them.

'Run!' shouts the Doctor, and you race for the monastery, hoping that you can somehow outrun three monsters!

If you go straight ahead, go to 53.

If you go to the left, go to 88.

The two werewolves let out bloodcurdling howls. You spot a chance to escape and you, the Doctor and Amy run for the exit. Once there, the path back to the TARDIS is much more dangerous, with gunshots and screams ringing in the evening air. There's an all-out battle between werewolves and soldiers going on!

'Can't we do something to help the people here?' you ask.

'We are,' insists the Doctor, 'by getting out of here and heading for where the wolves are congregating. There must be something that's causing all this.'

'You're just guessing again, aren't you?' asks Amy.

The Doctor gives a tight, serious smile and then you're in sight of the TARDIS – but there's a problem. An eight-foot-tall problem with slavering jaws of death is standing right by the Doctor's bizarre ship.

'It can't stay there forever, can it?' you ask from your hiding place. You look around and see a helicopter in the distance and point it out to the Doctor. 'If he's not going to move – and we could be found here any second – we could use that.'

The Doctor looks surprised. 'You can fly? You get flying lessons in school? Crikey. Your school is seriously cool.'

You shake your head. 'No, I thought you could! You're the one with the amazing time machine. A helicopter should be easy!'

The Doctor looks at the TARDIS and then the helicopter. Back and forth, hopping from one leg to the other.

'Or I could try to distract the werewolf?' you suggest.

'You decide!' says the Doctor.

If you decide to distract the werewolf, head to 10.

If you decide to take the helicopter, go to 90.

The girl in the pink crash helmet seems uninjured. She starts to murmur, 'Doctor...' You tell her that there's no need for a doctor, and that she's fine. That is until she wakes up properly and realises she and her friend crashed into a wolf monster!

You check on the man who suddenly leaps from the bike. Unclipping and whisking off his crash helmet in one smooth movement, he gives you a piercing gaze, looks you up and down and asks, 'You're not going to be in the way, are you?'

You don't know what to say as he runs around the bike to check on his friend. 'Amy! It's the Doctor! Are you okay?'

There are more groggy murmurings from the girl, Amy, and she tries to sit up.

'You need to wake up, Amy. There's a werewolf lying in the middle of the road where we ran into it. Not exactly how I wanted to meet one of these creatures again.'

With this he gives you a sharp look. 'What's your name?' You tell him and he replies, 'I'm the Doctor and this is Amy and that, over there, in a road in eastern Scotland, is – well, I think it is and if it's not we're in big trouble – what I once called a lupine haemovariform. But that's a bit of a mouthful so 'werewolf' will do. What I really mean to say is STAY BACK!'

You can barely take in everything he's saying. He smiles and then beams as Amy sits up. 'Good girl!' and then he reaches into a pocket in his tweed jacket and pulls out what looks like a bottle of perfume with an old-fashioned atomiser attached to it. You catch it as he throws it to you. 'It doesn't look like much but that's the best defence against this creature. Let's hope you don't have to use it.'

You look at the perfume bottle, then the Doctor, Amy, the motorbike and sidecar, the werewolf and the full moon in the cloudy sky. You realise that life has taken an exceptionally bizarre turn.

'Help me with the bike,' orders the Doctor, as he pulls the motorbike back onto the road. 'It's undamaged, which is a stroke of luck.'

As you help, he asks, 'The werewolf didn't get you, did it? You're not scratched or anything?'

You shake your head. 'Good, good,' the Doctor says, and then starts the bike's engine. 'Amy will be fine but we might need a quick getaway.'

You're surprised when he doesn't get on the bike. Instead, he turns on his heels and steps slowly towards the werewolf. You look at Amy who takes off her goggles and gives you a dazed smile.

If you decide to follow the Doctor to get a closer look at the werewolf and you have access to a computer, click on box D and enter the code word FOLLOW.

If you make this decision and do not have a computer, go to 29.

If you ask the Doctor who he and Amy are, go to 55.

You've never been so glad to reach home before. In the warmth of your room you realise the true meaning of the word 'safe'. Your mind races with what you've gone through. You've faced a real, live, actual werewolf... it's all you can think about. Everything at home seems so dull in comparison. You have some food, watch TV, and it's boring. Maybe you should've stayed to find out what was going on? At least you're home, at least you're safe.

Or so you think.

Within an hour or so of arriving home, a strange pulsing light passes through the room. You feel sick, dizzy and in tremendous pain – the room starts to spin as you fall to the floor. The last thing you know is that you're changing, growing taller and hairier, with claws extending from powerful hands. You're becoming a werewolf! Everything is blurry with confusion and pain. The thought 'There's no such thing as safe,' is your last. There's just one thing your new mind focuses on: Victory! The Empire of the Wolf begins tonight!

THE END

As you run past room after room, down brightly lit corridors, heading further into the base, the Doctor wishes that you'd all stayed together. 'I should never pay any attention to myself,' he says. 'There's something going on here. There must be a reason the werewolves and those ruins are here.'

In the base you're passed by lots of people, all looking worried. Some are armed soldiers and others in white coats look like scientists. You and the Doctor get odd glances but you're never stopped by anyone – they're all too busy worrying about their own skin to be worried about yours.

You turn a corner and see Amy – being terrorised by a werewolf! The Doctor fishes for something in his pocket but soldiers suddenly appear behind you, shout, 'DOWN!' and Amy dives at the Doctor's feet. They fire at the werewolf and in the long corridor the noise of the guns is deafening and terrifying. You can barely think; the din is turning your brain to mush. You can hardly keep your eyes open to see the Doctor pick up Amy.

The Doctor grabs your arm and pulls you away from the gunfight. You run! Round after round is fired behind you. If you've heard one shot you've heard a thousand. Then you hear human screaming and werewolf howling and you wish to never hear anything so horrible ever again.

'He was just this bloke,' says a stunned Amy. 'I saw him, injured, sat against the wall and wanted to help and then he changed.'

'Let's get out of here,' says the Doctor, looking at your ashen face.

'But you're here for a reason,' you insist. 'You said there was an explanation as to why the werewolves are here.'

'You're right. So do we stay to find out what it is?'

To find out more, go to 54.

To head for the exit, go to 69.

The Doctor throws dials, levers and switches on the TARDIS and you hear the sounds of massive, ancient-sounding engines. The noise fills the room and you see that the Doctor is holding onto the controls, while Amy holds onto a handrail — and then you discover why, when the room starts to sway one way and then the other. You reach for a handrail but the room suddenly spins and you're flat on your backside!

The massive column that had risen and fallen as the Doctor piloted his ship comes to a stop. Amy follows the Doctor as he heads for the doors, calling back, 'Are you going to stay there all night?'

Jumping up, you race after the two strangers to discover that you're somewhere completely different! Your disbelief that the box has moved is drowned out by the sound of alarms and soldiers in black uniforms running across what is clearly a military base. You see helicopters and army jeeps, and prefabricated buildings stacked in rows in front of an enormous warehouse.

Through all this you realise that you're looking for a werewolf — then realise the werewolf is probably what's causing all the alarm!

'We should split up,' suggests the Doctor.

'That always works so well,' says Amy, sarcastically. The Doctor smiles. 'Take this,' he says and passes Amy what looks like a thin leather wallet. 'If you get stuck, pretend you're someone important. Well, you are imp...' The Doctor stops himself. 'Never mind that. Have a look around. Don't get caught and locked up for any great length of time, please. If you see a werewolf, do not ask it what's on the dinner menu. Got that? Meet you back here in, say, twenty minutes?'

'Are we synchronising watches?' asks Amy.

The Doctor just gives Amy a look. 'Anyway,' he says, turning to you, 'which way are you going to go?'

If you go with the Doctor, go to 32.

If you want to go with Amy, go to 81.

You can't believe you're about to try to distract a three-metre-tall killer monster that you thought only existed in books and movies. Carefully you step forward, waving a large branch. This can't be any sort of plan! You're going to be eaten alive — and you turn to tell the Doctor this when you see two more werewolves step out from the base behind them. Your jaw drops. Amy and the Doctor turn and try to back away. They're trapped!

One of the monsters must be Professor Lazenby. All three of them come together and, incredibly, they ignore you! There is a terrific tremor and only the werewolves are left standing. As you pick yourself up from the damp ground, you see them howl at the moon and sprint off.

The Doctor, says, 'From that tremor, we don't have much time. The moon's near its zenith. Quick, into the TARDIS.'

You bundle inside the impossible machine and the Doctor bounds up to the central controls. 'Now,' he says, 'do we aim for the centre of the action or do you want to try and land outside?'

To land outside, go to 19.

To land in the centre, go to 27.

You can't hide from a werewolf! With heightened senses, they can sniff you out! You hear them stomp around the control room, smashing chairs and scattering all sorts of stuff. You desperately wish the Doctor would do something.

Then a werewolf is upon you! It howls in triumph. Then it lunges for you, swiping at your body – and that's the last thing you ever know!

THE END

You turn left sharply and skid on the road, coming off your bike. You're more or less unharmed and you've avoided the motorbike and sidecar. As you pick yourself up, you see the side of the motorbike slam into the werewolf, and it's thrown to one side. It lays still, its breathing fast and shallow.

You look in horror as the rider of the motorbike loses control and it and the sidecar plough into a fence at the roadside. Even though there's a giant creature lying in the middle of the road, your first thought is to help. You race over to the crashed bike and sidecar where the rider and passenger lie still. You see a man on the bike, his body lying over the handlebars and there's a woman in a pink crash helmet in the sidecar.

You look behind to see if the werewolf is coming round. It's not. Who do you check first?

If you check the woman first, go to 6.

If you check on the man first, go to 50.

The blast doors are coming down fast and you realise that it's now or never! You follow Amy rolling under the doors, with your coat almost getting trapped as the steel barrier slams down.

'Come on! We've got to follow her!' calls Amy over the blaring alarm. You see Dr Adams racing ahead. Picking yourself up, you start after her. You turn left, and right, again and again, sometimes having to turn back, the way blocked by a steel door and Adams has to find a different route. She isn't happy you're following, but there are more important things at stake – your lives!

You come to a massive control room where a computer screen dominates the far wall. It shows a map of the local area where a large red circle is pulsing. You recognise the area but more importantly, the Doctor is there, and he's arguing with a tall, dark-haired man who you think doesn't look well.

'How long have you known about the werewolves?' asks the Doctor.

The professor ignores him, and continues working at a console below the screen.

The Doctor says, 'From these readouts, you've focused on the exact wavelength to track the werewolves. How did you know that was even possible?'

'You're only hindering the operation here, Doctor,' says Lazenby without looking up. 'We'll contain the werewolves.'

'How do you know who I am? How long has this operation been

going on? Since 1879?'

This makes Lazenby look up.

'When Queen Victoria was almost infected? When the monks wanted to create the Empire of the Wolf?'

'You think you know so much,' sneers Lazenby. 'There was a maid at Torchwood House, who was cleaning up the blood and the infection passed on.'

'For more than a century it's been getting stronger again. And it's been passing on the infection. Now there are dozens of the things,' says the Doctor pointing at the map, 'meeting here.'

'It's the ruins of St Catherine's monastery,' you say.

'Of course! I wonder what the monks left behind, Professor?' The Doctor nods at Amy who's holding the psychic paper. She opens it up. Do you take a look?

If you do, go to 57.

If you don't, go to 82.

As you land you see the area around St Catherine's Glen lit up by the incredible light rising from the ruins of the monastery. You try to see the top of it but it goes on forever. You notice the moon will pass over it.

'You've spotted it too,' calls the Doctor over the noise of the helicopter. 'We don't have much time. I think when the moon passes through the light it'll trigger something...'

'Trigger what?' shouts Amy, keeping her long red hair down in the wind.

Before the Doctor can answer, he's interrupted by gunshots and the sound of werewolves howling on the other side of the ruins.

The pilot, Jackson, turns to you all. 'That sounds like our men need some help. I've got to give backup!'

That's just great, you think, but who'll protect you from the werewolves inside the ruins? They didn't have to both go! Surely the other soldier could've stayed?

As you stare at the ascending helicopter you hear a spine-melting howl that's far too close. The three of you turn to see three werewolves. They come slowly towards you.

Did you really have to get out of the helicopter? It was safer in there! But then, says a small voice in your mind, only until the moon passes into the light – then who knows what horror will be let loose!

There's only one place you can hide – the monastery ruins. There are two entrances.

To take the one straight in front of you, go to 53.

To take the one on the left, go to 88.

In a small, roofless room, you find a creature that's neither man nor werewolf, but a horrific mix of the two. You peer into a corner where it's hiding from the light. Its features seem to be shifting back and forth, as if something is holding back the transformation from man to monster.

'Are you Professor Lazenby?' asks the Doctor, walking towards him. 'You're astonishing. How are you resisting the haemovariform?'

The creature growls at him, 'Get back! You stink. Get back!'

The Doctor hurries to you and Amy. 'It can smell the mistletoe oil I'm carrying,' he says.

The creature sinks to its knees. 'I am Lazenby,' it insists in a gravelly voice. 'For how much longer, I don't know. The Wolf Stone calls me.'

The Doctor steps forward but Lazenby snarls, 'Don't come closer. The smell — it makes me angry.'

'What's wrong with the transformation?' asks the Doctor.

'Holding it back. Willpower. A trick I learned with the Brethren. And you're the Doctor from long ago. We thought you'd come. You were the enemy. You must stop it.'

'Stop what?'

'The Wolf Stone. The light. If the moon passes through the light, it'll be the end of everything. The Stone will have done its job.'

A wave of pain passes through Lazenby and, for a split second, it seems the werewolf within has won, but then his human side returns. The pain leaves Lazenby breathless.

'The infection, the werewolf curse,' he adds, 'it's a parasite. A mindless parasite. We thought we could control it. We learnt more about the wolf and the infection, trying to find ways to prevent and use the change. We found the Stone growing here. It was always here, underground, growing for centuries. Now it's too strong and we were too foolish.'

Amy says, 'Okay, think I've got it: the moon gets into the path of the light and the Wolf Stone, whatever that is, passes on the lupine wavelength haemo-doodah-form to everyone around Earth and so we're all werewolves. Dinner's on you? Yeah?'

You turn to the professor, but what do you ask?

To ask him how to stop the Wolf Stone, go to 25.

To ask how long he's been like this, go to 34.

If you have access to a computer, click on box B on screen and enter the code word NOW.

If you do not, read on.

You peer over the edge of the computers, when the room suddenly thrums and everything loose rattles or falls to the floor. The werewolves howl and stomp out of the room on their hind legs. You're safe — for now.

On the other side of the control room you find Amy and the Doctor emerging from their hiding place.

'That was some sort of signal, wasn't it?' you ask.

'Definitely — luckily for us,' says the Doctor. He stares at the computer screen with the map of the local area.

'It also means we're running out of time. I'm sure I'm missing something. Come on, come on, come on! What am I missing?'

What should the Doctor do?

If you think he should follow the werewolves in the TARDIS, go to 19.

If he should investigate further, go to 77.

You quickly turn your bike around. There's a bad feeling in your gut and you recognise the sensation — it's the dark, hollow feeling of fear. You know there's something wrong with the thing on the road. But you know half a dozen shortcuts home. Perhaps you can find one before it reaches you!

You take a look behind you to see the creature is racing after you! You're so surprised you almost stop the bike but your flight-or-fight response kicks in and you pedal like someone possessed. As the blood pumps around your body, your heartbeat getting faster, your breathing getting harder, all you think you can hear is the fast and heavy footfalls of the thing behind you. You've barely time to wonder what it could be.

You take another look — it's getting closer! You re-double your efforts. You've never cycled so hard in your life. It's now that you hear the sound of the motorbike. You flash your head round to see the motorbike and sidecar coming up behind the beast and you.

Terrified, you look at the animal bounding towards you. You see it caught in the moonlight — it's a giant wolf creature! A mad thought passes through your mind: wolves haven't lived in the British Isles since at least the 18th century! What's one doing here now? More importantly, why's it chasing you?

You spot a narrow alleyway. You could possibly ride your bike through it, and it's narrow enough that it should slow the wolf creature down or even stop it!

If you think the alley is too narrow for your bike, go to 62.

If you decide to go down the alley, go to 75.

'What do you hope to achieve with a pack of werewolves on the loose?' asks the Doctor. 'I mean, those creatures are wild. They're non-containable three-metre-tall walking fur-balls of rage. What do you think the army can do with that? They can't be tamed.'

Lazenby listens to the Doctor and then laughs sharply. 'The army? Doctor, you're slipping. This isn't the army. Oh, we've been funded by Her Majesty's Government but we're not the army. This isn't like your friends at UNIT.'

'No, they'd have shut this down and slaughtered the werewolves, too, forgetting there are human beings under that fur.'

'Compassionate as I've been told,' said Lazenby.

'Who told you?'

'This, Doctor,' says Lazenby, spreading his arms wide, 'this is the Brethren of the Wolf.'

You ask, 'What's the Brethren of the Wolf?'

'The last time I ran into them they were a bunch of martial artists in fetching red robes and shaven heads worshipping the werewolf and wanting to use it to take over the British Empire.' The Doctor looks around. 'You've moved with the times. Still wanting to take over the world? I'll have to stop you.'

'You think you can?'

'If I don't, you won't stop the werewolves.'

'The rogue creatures will be contained. That's nothing for you to worry about.'

You see a phone. Could it be a lifeline? You hear the Doctor and Lazenby argue about 'Torchwood House', how a maid was infected cleaning up after the werewolf and how the Brethren had twisted the werewolf's purpose on Earth. As you crouch behind a workstation, you hear Lazenby announce that, after tonight, every human being on the planet will be a werewolf!

You grab the phone.

If you phone the police, go to 52.

If you call your family, go to 86.

If you have access to a computer, click on box C on screen and enter the code word TARDIS.

If you do not, read on.

In the TARDIS, the Doctor races around the amazing machine in the centre of the room, flicking switches, slamming levers, checking dials and with a cry of, 'Hold on!' you hear the noise of engines coming to life. You grab a hand-rail and see that Amy is doing the same, as the Doctor flips from one part of the console to another. The column that rises and falls in time with the engine noise begins to slow and then stops.

'Ding-ding! Werewolf Central!' says the Doctor.

'Do you have to be so happy about it?' asks Amy.

'I could do the terrified thing if you want,' says the Doctor heading for the doors. 'Come on, you two. I've checked the scanner. There's no immediate danger — but don't expect that to last long.'

You follow Amy and the Doctor. In the moonlight you see that the TARDIS is now in the middle of a field. You're surrounded by boggy land. In the distance you see the ruins of an old building you recognise.

'That's the old monastery,' you tell the Doctor. 'It was abandoned years ago.'

The Doctor is intrigued. 'Of course, the monks — the Brethren — they worshipped the wolf that wanted to infect Queen Victoria. They were here. What if they left something behind?'

He marches on and you and Amy race over the sodden ground to keep up.

'Shouldn't we be a little more careful?' asks Amy.

The Doctor points straight up to the sky. 'From the moon's path, we don't have much time.'

As if on cue, a massive beam of white light shoots skywards and there's howling from a multitude of werewolves. Their noise sends shivers down your spine. Some howls were very close indeed. You turn around to see three werewolves heading straight for you!

'Run!' shouts the Doctor — but which way should you go?

To go straight on, go to 53.

To go left, go to 88.

You scrabble around, desperate to find something, anything that could beat back the monster when the man on the motorbike shouts, 'Oi!' You turn to him to hear him shout, 'Catch!' as he throws something like a screwdriver at you. You leap to catch it. It's a piece of funny-looking plastic! What use is this?

'Point the thin end at the werewolf and press the top button, NOW!'

In your nervous state you fumble at the device, almost dropping it, but you do what he says. You're not prepared for what happens next. The gadget emits the most jaw-dropping, tear-inducing piercing noise you've ever heard. The air is thick with the sound and it's hard to believe such a deafening din could come from a device so small.

The reaction from the creature is immediate and it howls in pain, its ears flatten against its head – which would be comical if the thing wasn't a werewolf that, seconds earlier, was about to attack you! The sound drives the monster wild and its hearing must be more sensitive than yours because it curls up on the ground, unable to move.

Then you remember the man and woman in the bike and sidecar. They could be injured.

To go over to the people by the bike, go to 6.

To keep using the gadget on the werewolf, go to 84.

Amy's behaviour changes suddenly, becoming cold and distant. She flashes the wallet at the woman and tells her that she's Amy Munroe, part of the new medical team and that you are the 'latest subject'.

'I'm Dr Rachel Adams,' says the woman, who seems to have been won over by Amy's performance and the psychic paper. She looks at you. 'I take it the infection is recent?'

'That's right. I'm just going to the, erm, control centre.'

'Really? Professor Lazenby won't be happy. Normally, the subjects are kept in isolation and processed. It's lucky the subject's not so far advanced that it hasn't turned wolf already.'

She starts walking ahead of you, away from the room full of cages. You and Amy share a look of 'I don't know what we're doing, but let's do it anyway and hope for the best'.

Dr Adams marches on, talking all the time. 'It's complete bedlam out there. Our two subjects have escaped and we've discovered there are at least another forty of the creatures in the area. Can you believe that? Forty! Where the blazes did they come from?'

This isn't news to you, but you're shocked that it seems the situation with the werewolves is out of the military's control. If there are forty to fifty werewolves in the area then what chance do the three of you have?

'And what did you intend to do with the subjects?' asks Amy.

Dr Adams spins sharply on her heels to face Amy and you all stop.

'They plan to make an army.' She peers hard at your newfound friend. 'But you didn't know that, did you? Just who are you? Let me see that identification again.'

At that moment, the Doctor appears behind Dr Adams. You and Amy shout out 'Doctor!' in surprise. Dr Adams turns to see who it is and you take the opportunity to use the distraction to push her out of the way and into the wall. 'Run!' you shout and you race up the corridor the Doctor has just come down.

'I did tell you about the running, didn't I?' asks the Doctor as you pelt up one corridor, taking a left, another left, then a right in a desperate bid to lose Dr Adams.

'We should try to get out of here!' shouts Amy.

'Then it's lucky we're heading the right way!' cries the Doctor. 'But don't you want to find out what's going on?'

If you want to find out if the base can tell you more about the werewolves, go to 69.

If you think you've found out enough, go to 54.

The Doctor leaves the TARDIS first — to be faced with a roaring werewolf that appears from nowhere! You push the Doctor out of its way only to be confronted by the monster yourself! It swipes at you and, as you lift your hands to protect yourself, the creature's claws scratch your skin. It burns!

Suddenly, the monster backs away as the Doctor furiously sprays mistletoe oil at it. The werewolf roars in anger before running off.

The Doctor examines the scratches. 'Are you okay?' he asks.

'No,' is the simple answer. You can feel the haemovariform coming alive inside you as the blood pumps through your body. You're becoming a werewolf!

Then another creature comes in but this one is strange — it's half human, half werewolf and all terrifying! It roars at you and then sinks to its knees. 'I am not a monster! I'm Professor Lazenby!'

You can't believe what you're seeing but the pain is immense. You feel the werewolf taking over your mind. The change is imminent.

If you ask the Lazenby creature, 'Is there a way to cure the werewolves?' go to 68.

If you ask it, 'Is there a way to stop becoming a werewolf?' go to 76.

You're surprised when the Doctor raises his hands and meekly allows himself to be Lazenby's prisoner. 'It doesn't have to be like this you know, Professor. I'm sure we could sort this out amicably.'

'Take them to the cage room,' Lazenby orders two soldiers. Their obedience is immediate. They grab you and the Doctor by the shoulders and start pushing you out of the doorway.

'There is nothing to 'sort out' except you,' adds Lazenby. 'And with you locked away in the toughest cages known to man, I think that's you dealt with.'

'See you soon, Professor,' says the Doctor and you're both taken down one long corridor after another until you arrive at the cage room. 'I've lost count of the times I've been incarcerated, imprisoned, confined. But I don't think I've ever been caged before.'

If you have access to a computer, click on box F on screen and type in the code word CAGE.

If you do not, read on.

The surly, silent soldiers open two cages with electronic locks. You're bundled inside and they leave.

'This must be where they wanted to keep the werewolves,' muses the Doctor, sitting cross-legged on the cage floor. 'What did Lazenby hope to achieve? You can't tame a terror like the haemovariform. A ray of moonlight and that's it, the beast overcomes the brain. The werewolf has an unquenchable hunger, spreading itself and devouring all it can.'

'How do we get out?'

'With this,' he says, fishing out a strange pen-like device. 'It's my sonic screwdriver. Opens anything. Nine times out of ten. Well, eight times out of ten...'

'What about Amy?'

'Amy!' the Doctor cries. 'Step back!' he orders, aiming the sonic screwdriver at your cage. There's a series of sparks and the cage door swings open. He does the same to his own cage.

'Now, which way?' he asks.

To go right, go to 32.

To go left, go to 64.

By the broken wall you watch the battle between the soldiers and the werewolf in fascination. The monster grows angrier with every bullet that hits it, but you know it won't die, while the soldiers are certain to.

You're about to shout at the soldiers to run for their lives when your view is blocked – by another werewolf! You shout out in shock and terror at its sudden appearance. As you turn to run, it lashes out with its huge claws. You feel a sharp sting on your back and you fall to the floor.

The Doctor races over, madly spraying mistletoe oil which enrages the creature and it's driven away.

'Are you all right?' asks Amy, crouching over you.

It doesn't look good! The Doctor checks your back and the skin has been broken. You can feel the haemovariform coming alive in your body. It's coursing through your veins like fire. You can hear your heart pumping the blood, its beat getting faster and stronger.

'Am I going to become a werewolf?' you ask.

'Not if I can help it!' says the Doctor.

The werewolf reappears and roars at you all. The Doctor fumbles with the perfume bottle but just as he's about to spray mistletoe oil, the creature grows smaller and becomes less hairy – it's turning back into a human being! Even as the pain in your body increases, you can't help but wonder what's happening. Has this creature passed on the infection and cured himself?

But the transformation doesn't complete. The figure before you is in considerable pain as it hovers between monster and man. 'I am not a werewolf!' it cries. 'I am Professor Lazenby!'

All you can think about is becoming a werewolf.

If you ask if there's a way to cure the werewolves, go to 68.

If you ask the professor if there is a way to stop becoming a werewolf, go to 76.

Lazenby's features shift between human and werewolf as you ask if he knows how to stop the signal. His eyeballs turn black, then return to normal, but his irises flicker from brown to bright blue. He closes his eyes and you can see that it's taking a monumental effort to retain control of his humanity. His features become almost human and when he opens his eyes again, they're normal but filled with sadness.

'There's only one way for sure,' he says in a growl. He finds it difficult to stand and the Doctor helps him to his feet. Slowly, Lazenby leads you towards the light.

You gasp as you enter a large room that's open to the sky. There are dozens of werewolves lying on the floor, all facing a large odd-looking platform from which the huge column of light extends into the night. For a moment you're mesmerised.

The Doctor wants to race over to the podium but Lazenby holds him back.

'Just wait,' he says.

You doubt that you'll ever see anything as weird as werewolves looking like they're praying. The column's radiance bleaches colour from the room. Everything looks monochrome, but the more you stare at the massive shaft of light the more you see strange coloured patterns whirling around.

'What are we waiting for?' you ask.

'The fifty seeds are here,' says Lazenby, in his rumbling voice. Before you can ask what he means, he looks at you with sad eyes and says, 'I wanted to control this. I thought I could use this power. But it's used me.'

A beam shoots from the column of light and somehow picks up a werewolf from the ground. Then another, then another. The lifted werewolves glow a brilliant white and their form changes to human.

'Look at the beams of light,' says Amy, pointing at the beams where swirling purple strands emerge from the monsters' bodies. 'Something's being pulled from them.'

'It's the werewolf part of them,' says the Doctor. 'The stone must need a critical mass of werewolf DNA. Lazenby! What have you done? We need to stop this!'

You see every wolf monster has been lifted off the ground and then Lazenby is hit by a beam of light. You, the Doctor and Amy race over to the stone platform but Lazenby calls out, 'It's too late for you to do anything,' and he pulls out the Doctor's bottle of mistletoe oil – he must have picked the Doctor's pocket when he needed help to stand!

Pulling off the top, Lazenby drinks the oil and screams!

'No!' shouts the Doctor. 'You don't have to do this!'

Suddenly you hear the stone platform crack, the light column is extinguished and you're plunged into darkness! You've got spots before your eyes. There's utter silence until the Doctor says, 'Everyone stay exactly where they are!'

Your eyes adjust to the moonlit gloom and all around you are naked people stirring on the ground. The Doctor makes his way over to Lazenby – he's dead. 'You didn't have to do this,' whispers the Doctor, kneeling at the brave man's body.

All of a sudden you're aware of the sound of running, booted footsteps and helicopters – soldiers! And they're coming towards you!

'Time we made ourselves scarce, Doctor,' says Amy, her hand placed gently on the Doctor's shoulder.

He stands up and turns, a sad but resolute look on his face. 'You're right. Come on, Pond.'

'What about me?' you ask.

'It's time you went home, isn't it?'

'Sure,' you say. 'I guess.'

The Doctor smiles. 'But how about taking the scenic route?'

THE END

You answer as honestly as you can: 'The last time we saw him he was outside, looking for the werewolf.'

Dr Adams seems happy with your reply. 'Good,' she says, 'I'm glad you told the truth. I can always spot a liar. Seeing as we're in the cage room, you might as well stay here while I find Professor Lazenby and warn him about the Doctor.'

If you have access to a computer, click on box F on screen and enter the code word HIDE.

If you do not, read on.

Ordering you inside, Adams uses a metal card to activate the electronic locks on two of the cages. You're trapped – but not for long. As soon as Adams is clear of the cage room, Amy shows you an identical metal card and frees herself.

'Maybe I should leave you in there. You might be less likely to cause trouble,' she smiles.

'Where did you get that from?' you ask.

'Swiped it earlier. I'm terrible for picking pockets!'

'Come on! Get it open!' you hiss at her. 'If we follow her we can find this professor and find out what's going on.'

Amy swipes your cage lock and you're free. Luckily, you're soon in sight of Dr Adams, who is striding purposefully through the base's brightly lit and sterile corridors. You follow her to a large control room – and the Doctor's already there, arguing with Dr Adams and a tall, dark-haired, ill-looking man who can only be Professor Lazenby.

You and Amy sneak into the room carefully.

'–red pulses on the map here,' says the Doctor, pointing at a massive screen that dominates the room, 'you've tuned them into the lupine wavelength haemovariform. How did you manage that? How did you even know to do that?'

He sees you and Amy come into the room and gives a slight nod, then mimes opening something.

You hear Lazenby's deep, rich voice tell the Doctor that 'the haemovariform never died out on Earth. They're easy to track. We've been hoping to create an army of the wolves but this latest phase of the moon has made them uncontrollable. We're going to wipe them out.'

'What? You can't!' The Doctor is appalled. 'They're people, too!'

'If the werewolf inside them cannot be controlled, then they're useless. This whole operation is forfeit.'

You see Amy fish out the psychic paper and guess this was what the Doctor was miming. Do you take a peek at what it says?

If you sneak a peek, go to 57.

If you think it might be personal, go to 82.

The TARDIS comes to a halt with a thud and the central column that had been rising and falling stops. All you can hear is a background hum. The Doctor and Amy are quiet, looking at each other and then at the doors which lead to who knows where.

'Scanner!' cries the Doctor, quickly pulling down an odd-looking TV from over the centre of the TARDIS. He thumps it on the side. Something rattles. 'That used to work. I used to thump the TARDIS all the time. Perhaps my aim is a bit off.'

'So,' you say, 'no scanner.'

'Nope. Step out of those doors and who knows what could be out there.'

'My money's on werewolves. Lots of them.' This is from Amy. 'All ready to eat us up.'

'Mistletoe!' cries the Doctor again, and you don't know what to think. He suddenly pulls up a section of the floor to reveal a large wooden chest with the letter 'M' ornately engraved on it. Opening it, he rummages through a collection of bizarre odds and ends, muttering, 'Dried marsh fruit, marriage certificate, key of Marinus,' then stands up and cries, 'Mistletoe oil!'

He holds up an old-fashioned perfumed bottle, then sprays himself with the contents. 'Come here,' he says. As you and Amy step forward, he sprays you with the oddly scented and sticky oil too.

'Trust me,' he says. 'Werewolves hate this stuff.'

The oil is tacky to the touch and it's in your hair and on your clothes. It's got in your nose and is all you can taste and smell now!

'Don't pull that face,' says the Doctor, 'I just might have saved your life. This could protect you—'

'Only 'could'?' asks Amy.

'Nothing in this life is guaranteed, Amy.'

'Apart from being in mortal peril at least twice an hour with you.'

'No domestics, please, Ms Pond. We have a guest.' He smiles at you. 'As I was saying, this could protect you from werewolves because the last one I met hated this stuff. And I mean hated it with a passion. Like me and apples. And yoghurt.'

With that, he walks to the TARDIS doors and you and Amy follow. Slowly and carefully, he opens them to peek outside.

If you want to be the first to leave the TARDIS, go to 40.

If the Doctor is first to leave, go to 22.

There are dozens of werewolves lying on the floor, all arranged in a circle around the immense column of light. Surely it'd be madness to walk through these vicious killers? You hang back, watching the Doctor and Amy step carefully towards a huge platform, the source of the pillar of light. You realise the werewolves have ignored them. Are the creatures in some sort of trance?

You hear heavy animal breathing from behind you and turn to see three werewolves on all fours padding towards you! In unison, they rear up on their back legs and roar at you. One swipes at you and you stumble backwards. All seems lost – you're lying on the ground face to face with a werewolf! – when the air is filled with a dreadful noise. Clasping your hands to your ears, you turn to see it's the Doctor pointing a gadget in your direction. The sound is incredible and its effect is astounding.

All the werewolves that had lain prone on the floor rise up and the place is filled with the roaring of wild and furious monsters. The shrieking from the Doctor's gadget continues and the creatures can't cope with it. They flee into the countryside. But the sound affects the pillar of light, too. Sparks and smoke erupt from the stone at its base. The light flickers and dies. It takes a moment to adjust to the gloom but you soon cheer when you realise the light has stopped and the werewolves have gone!

'You did it, Doctor!' you shout.

But the Doctor looks as angry as a werewolf. 'Not at all – all the werewolves here were people too. I might have saved you, but that means they're still werewolves. They could still spread the haemovariform.'

You hear sounds of shooting in the distance. 'It seems they're already being tracked down,' he adds with a terrible sadness in his voice. 'It's an end, but it's not how it should've been. Come on, Pond. It's time we left. Will you be okay getting home?'

You nod, still in shock. And with that they turn and walk away.

THE END

If you have access to a computer, click on box D on screen and type in the code word FOLLOW.

If you do not, read on.

The Doctor carefully walks over to the prone body of the werewolf. It seems to have been knocked out from the collision with the Doctor's motorbike. He doesn't even look up at you as you approach him and the monster. He just holds out a flat palm and says, quietly and clearly, 'I thought I told you to stay back. I know I did. I definitely did.' Then he looks at you and suddenly you feel a different kind of fear. It might be because you're having the craziest night of your life, but your instincts are saying that this man, this Doctor, is even more dangerous than the werewolf.

He flashes a huge smile and suddenly everything is all right in the world. If you have to deal with a monster, you have a feeling this man can sort it out.

He pulls out a test tube from a pocket and a pair of tweezers. 'We gave you quite a thump, didn't we?' he asks the prone werewolf, which doesn't reply. 'But with what I suspect to be an alien physiognomy overwriting human DNA, you'll be regenerating faster than I can.'

And with that the Doctor plucks a long, thick, grey hair from the monster's body – which then stirs and starts to sit up! You and the Doctor quickly back away. But which vehicle do you head for?

If you run for your own bike, go to 17.

If you jump on the Doctor's motorbike, go to 74.

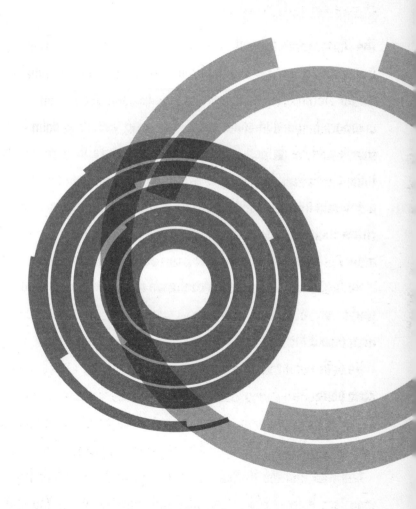

Amy pulls away from you and rolls under the barrier, shouting at you to do the same. But you hesitate too long and the doors slam down, leaving you trapped! You hear Amy slamming her fists against the steel door but to no avail.

You hear a muffled cry that you think sounds something like 'I'll get the Doctor!' You hear running footsteps and then all is silent.

You wait. You wait some more. You bang your fists on the walls, shouting to be let out. But no one comes. More time passes when suddenly a bright light washes over the room. You feel nauseous and are wracked with a sudden terrible pain! What's happening to you? Through blurred vision you see that you're changing: your arms are growing longer and hairier, with giant paws instead of hands, ending in terrible claws. All you feel is confusion and agony and you're losing control of your mind. Then, just as suddenly, it's over. You're still trapped but there's one thing your new mind can focus upon: Victory! The Empire of the Wolf begins tonight!

THE END

You instinctively hurl yourself at the werewolf, knowing that you're probably going to end up dead, but you have to protect the Doctor somehow. After grappling with the wolf monster for what feels like forever but is only seconds, the creature roars at you, its saliva splattering your face. It knocks you back with an outstretched claw which tears at your skin. You land in a heap on the floor and can feel the alien infection coursing through your body!

But the werewolf hasn't finished with you. It's not going to let you join the ranks of the haemovariform. The look in its eyes is clear – it means to kill you! Amy picks up a chair and throws it at the monster stomping over to you. As your vision starts to blur, you see the Doctor working furiously at the computer. Have you bought him enough time?

There's a tremendous BOOM in the distance and you pass out – but only for a moment. When you revive, the Doctor and Amy are crouched over you, wondering if you're all right – and you are! You can't feel a trace of the infection any more.

'I wasn't one hundred per cent certain that the cancellation signal would work,' says the Doctor. 'And it's hard to type fast when you've got all your fingers crossed! If it hadn't been for your bravery, the werewolf might have killed us all, and then I'd never have sent the signal. You just saved the world.'

You sit up and smile, finding it hard to take everything in. All you can say is, 'Wow!'

'But now,' says the Doctor, 'it's time to take you home.'

Your face falls.

The Doctor smiles. 'But how about going the long way round in the TARDIS?' He helps you to your feet. 'Come on!'

THE END

Sneaking around the base's grounds is child's play for you and the Doctor. You dart from building to building, getting closer to the main base with every step. There are plenty of armed soldiers around, but they seem far too busy trying to find the cause of the alarm – which you realise is likely to be the werewolf that the Doctor spotted on the TARDIS scanner!

'Where are we going?' you ask.

'Inside there,' says the Doctor, pointing to the main building.

'What's in there?'

'Answers, I hope.' With that, he dashes off, leaving you to race after him.

There are amber lights flashing around the base, making every shadow cast a strange one. You try your best to quell your fear as you near the main building. There's a monster on the loose, you're about to break into a military building and you're doing it with a man who has a blue box that can somehow pick itself up and land somewhere else...

Soon you're at the front of the base. There are two tall thick glass doors announcing 'UNAUTHORISED ENTRY FORBIDDEN'. You're surprised there are no guards. The Doctor waves something that looks like a screwdriver at the door but it acts like a remote control. There's a spark as electronic locks are disabled and the doors swing open.

You're about to step inside when two soldiers burst out, pointing rifles at you and the Doctor. You both raise your hands to heaven in surrender when you suddenly hear an all-too-familiar roar behind you. It's the werewolf!

'Down!' shouts the Doctor and he pushes you down and forward, past the legs of the soldiers who start shooting at the beast. You hear the Doctor shout, 'Get inside!' as bullets are fired and the monster roars. You hurtle into the base, not daring to look behind you. Which way do you go now?

If you decide to go right, go to 8.

If you go left, go to 64.

Werewolves? Real, live werewolves? You've no doubt: you don't want to miss any of this. After being handed an old-fashioned perfume bottle ('You may need this,' says the Doctor) and a helmet from under the bike's seat, you ride pillion with the Doctor while Amy climbs into the sidecar.

The vehicle speeds off. You enjoy the feeling of the wind in your face, but it soon gets a bit cold. But does it matter? You're hunting werewolves!

You realise you don't know where you're going as the Doctor tears down the road. You have to shout to ask him where you're heading.

He shouts back, 'Balmoral!'

'The Queen's castle? She's not here. She's only here in summer. Usually. I think,' you shout. 'Why there?'

'There have been werewolf sightings over the last few months in this area,' he calls back, 'always at the full moon. The last time I faced the werewolf, it was a big fan of the royal family. I have a feeling they might be involved.'

'Really?'

'Really!'

After seeing a werewolf, you're prepared to believe almost anything but you continue the ride in silence, thinking over what you've seen this evening. That the Doctor has faced a werewolf before fills you with confidence – he lived to tell the tale, then!

You pass a field that's littered with the ruins of an old abandoned monastery. The basic building is still standing, although it's missing its roof. It's always puzzled you why no one's torn it down. You're shocked when a gigantic column of light shoots up into the evening sky.

The Doctor brakes hard and your two crash helmets crack together. 'Oof!'

'Sorry!' cries the Doctor as he steps off the bike. You step off too, and help Amy out of the sidecar. The three of you walk towards the light. The chances of this having nothing to do with the werewolf is remote, you realise.

'Now that is impressive,' says the Doctor.

'Any idea what it's for?'

'A signal of some kind? How far does the light go up? Can you see the–' He stops short. 'Look,' he says, pointing to the moon that's crossing the cloudy sky. 'The moon's path goes directly across the light.' He turns to you. 'Where are we?'

He's not surprised by your answer. 'The Brethren's monastery!' he exclaims, leading to looks of incomprehension from you and Amy.

'What's the Brethren?' she asks, a split second before you do just the same.

'This cult that helped the werewolf when I met it. Worshipped it. This place must've been theirs. Did they leave something behind?'

'You're saying the werewolf's alien?' you ask.

'Didn't I say? Absolutely it's alien. Landed here, probably, hundreds of years ago. Found a host, went from body to body, growing stronger over the centuries and then it met me. Uh-oh.'

The Doctor's story stops and he's looking over the shoulders of you and Amy. Slowly, with a cold fist of fear forming in your stomach, you dare yourself to turn around. Behind you is not one werewolf, but three — all looking ravenous.

You turn back to the Doctor and see that the monastery ruins has two entrances. Which one should you take?

To take the entrance in front of you, go to 52.

To take the entrance on the right, go to 88.

The half-werewolf creature calling itself Lazenby says, 'I've been like this all of my life. The curse has been passed down from generation to generation. The other creatures here are from all over the world. Each one of us descended from that poor cleaning maid at Torchwood House all those years ago.'

'What are you all here for?' asks the Doctor.

He looks at the Doctor with pain in his eyes. Controlling the transformation is taking almost all his effort.

'The Wolf Stone. It's been calling us. It's been singing, screaming, howling — ever since the last full moon. The Brethren thought they could control it but they just couldn't. It's been waiting for tonight for so, so long.'

The man is wracked with a sudden blast of pain. 'No!' he cries. 'I am Professor Lazenby! I am not a monster!' But it seems that the professor is about to become a werewolf once more.

'We need to go, Doctor. He could turn any second!' says Amy.

'Lazenby!' says the Doctor, shaking the half-man, half-werewolf creature. 'What's the Wolf Stone going to do?'

The professor puts his hands to his head. You see his eyes flicker from normal brown to werewolf blue. The eyeballs turn black, and then become normal again. 'I can't hold on... the power of the moon... the singing of the stone — it's hurting me!' And he screams.

Right before your eyes he transforms almost instantaneously! The

Doctor pulls you away but the werewolf swipes at you, its claws cutting your arm. You suddenly feel dizzy. What should you do?

If you run from the werewolf, go to 83, or if you have access to a computer, click on box A on screen and enter the code word RUN.

If you hide from the werewolf, go to 37.

'There might be an off switch,' says the Doctor. 'The trick is just finding it.'

You look at the strange stone, and at how the crystals and flesh merge. The crystals are all dull and could be almost any colour, but everything is bleached out under the fantastic column of light. Deep inside it, however, you think you can see a blood-red light pulsing like a heartbeat, but with the room so dazzlingly bright, you can't be sure.

You realise you're staring at the stone and then notice the Doctor is doing exactly the same. You hope that he's working it out better than you are, because you can't make neither head nor tail of the strange device, and you tell the Doctor this.

'Then I'll tell you,' he says. 'From what we've gathered so far, I think this needs a certain amount of werewolf DNA, which activates a transmitter which sends out a gene re-sequencing wave that, more or less, copies what the lupine wavelength haemovariform does to human beings.'

'So, you mean it turns us all into monsters?' translates Amy.

A sudden beam of light shoots out from the main column and, amazingly, it picks up one of the werewolves. The creature glows brightly and its body lies limp. Through the light you can see the werewolf features fade — it's turning back into a human being. The

Doctor was right – the Wolf Stone is extracting the werewolf DNA!

You notice that there's a new noise in the room. It's the Wolf Stone and it sounds like it's powering up.

Another werewolf is picked up, then another and another.

'We're running out of time, Doctor!' says Amy.

The Doctor decides to try a more manual approach to investigating the Wolf Stone and goes to press one of the crystals sticking out of the strange flesh. As he touches it, he pulls back. 'That hurt!'

'Is it electrified?'

'Better than that,' says the Doctor. 'It doesn't like the mistletoe oil on my fingers!'

He pulls his perfume bottle out of his pocket.

If you stop the Doctor spraying the oil, go to 56.

If Amy stops him, go to 63.

You scrabble for something on the ground, anything at all, but there's nothing you can find to hit the werewolf with. This is it! The werewolf roars and lunges forward about to strike. You cover your eyes as the monster is about to deliver the fatal blow, when you hear a desperate yowl and realise that you're being sprayed with something perfumed and sticky!

You open your eyes to see a man in a bow tie standing over you with an old-fashioned atomiser perfume bottle in his hands, squirting madly at the werewolf – which races off!

You thank him as he helps you to stand. 'No need to thank me. I wasn't even sure mistletoe oil was going to work. Still that's that theory tested, isn't it? They're rather allergic to it, aren't they?'

You know the man is talking perfect English but what's coming out of his mouth doesn't make any sense.

'What theory? What are you talking about?'

'Ah, I've met this particular type of werewolf before.' This makes you raise your eyebrow. 'And the last time I thought it had been trained to avoid mistletoe but it's obviously much more fundamental than that. I'm just sorry that the only chance to test this was in saving your life.' This makes you raise the other eyebrow.

You're distracted as the red-haired woman walks over, taking off her lurid-pink crash helmet as she does so. They're unharmed from the crash. 'I'm Amy, this is the Doctor. We've been chasing that werewolf ever since the moon came up.'

This sounds like madness to you, but you're too polite to say so. The Doctor, who has darted off and is examining the ground, shouts, 'Here!' and picks up a few long, thick strands of hair and puts them in a test tube he finds in his pocket. 'I'll be able to track it much better now in the TARDIS.'

'Wouldn't it be easier to just jump on the bike and go after it?' you ask.

If you fancy riding pillion with the Doctor and chasing the werewolf, go to 47.

If you want to know what a TARDIS is, go to 78.

The Doctor and Amy pull you out of the room and hide! You can hear Lazenby howl as he transforms into the monster — and you're going to become one, too. You feel dizzy and nauseous, like you've eaten too many cakes. Amy checks the broken skin on your body and her fingers brush across a scratch which makes you shout out loud.

'Sorry!' says Amy. 'What did I do?'

'Keep it down! We don't want Lazenby finding us,' says the Doctor. You strain to hear any approaching footsteps but can hear nothing. After a moment he adds, 'Let me look at that scratch.'

You show him the torn flesh and see that where Amy touched it is inflamed. 'This is going to sting,' says the Doctor and he touches the scratch, too. You almost jump out of your skin the pain is so intense.

'I thought so,' says the Doctor. 'Where you've been hurt is sensitive to mistletoe oil. It's reacting to the haemovariform cells in the cut.'

You can barely make out what he's saying, you're feeling so spaced out. You just want the sensation to stop. It's all you can think about.

The Doctor gets out the perfume bottle. 'Now this really is going to sting. More than anything in the world. Are you ready?'

Dazed, you nod your head and the second the Doctor sprays your body, your vision turns red. There is nothing in your world but pain — until a few seconds later you start to feel your head clear.

'I've only bought you a little time, that's all. We've got to stop that

Wolf Stone transmitting its signal otherwise every human being on the planet is doomed, not just you.'

Suddenly you hear shooting, the sound of helicopters and orders being shouted out.

If you ignore it and head for the Wolf Stone, go to 83, or if you have access to a computer, click on box A on screen and enter the code word RUN.

To find out who it is, go to 92.

You barely breathe as you wind your way through the werewolves, but not a single one of them stirs as you reach the stone platform. There's a feeling of immense relief when you reach the Doctor's side. Here the pillar of light is dazzling. At its base is what you assume must control it. At first glance you think it's made of stone, but it seems almost flesh-like, and there are strangely shaped crystals protruding from it.

Something catches the corner of your eye and you turn to see three more werewolves stride in. Your heart plunges into your stomach with fear until you see them fall to the floor, joining their comrades. There's a deep chime that seems to come from the stone, making the floor reverberate.

'What was that?' you ask. 'The dinner gong?'

'I think this thing is ready. Look,' says the Doctor, 'the moon is passing into the light's path. The werewolves need to be here. They're part of this. The mechanism. Whatever this light is going to do, it needs the werewolves. But what for?'

'What about the last time you faced the werewolf?' asks Amy.

'That was on its own, using a human cult obsessed with the werewolf. Nothing like this. It wanted to create an Empire of the Wolf. But why wasn't this stone part of the plan back then?'

'Was it here, then?'

'That could be it! When the lupine wavelength haemovariform

came to Earth, it crashed. A single cell survived, infected a human host and grew stronger. What if this stone thing crashed here, too, and did the same, growing all this time? Waiting for the right moment to create the Empire of the Wolf.' The Doctor's face falls. 'I think it's a transmitter.'

'Radio Rip Out Your Heart 106.2FM?' says Amy.

'Worse than that – I think it's a DNA re-sequencer. If I'm right, this machine will turn every human on Earth into a werewolf!'

A beam is fired out from the column of light, hitting a werewolf and lifting it up in mid-air, making the creature glow.

'I don't know exactly what's happening,' says the Doctor, 'so don't ask!'

As you watch, more werewolves are picked up by new beams of light and you see that the figures glow and lose their werewolf features to become human.

To suggest smashing the crystal, go to 45.

To suggest pulling the bodies out of the light beams, go to 60.

You ask, 'What about the army?'

'That's brilliant!' cries the Doctor.

'What is?' shouts Amy from the sidecar.

'There's an army base about… umm… three miles that way,' he replies, and turns the bike to the right.

'The army?' Amy's surprise is obvious. 'You don't *do* army. You hate armies.'

'I'm going to have to make an exception. The three of us shouldn't go up against fifty werewolves.'

Three miles over bumpy moor takes longer than you'd like, but you're glad to be further away from the werewolves. But you think every shadow you see in the distance is another monster. The Doctor says there are fifty. Could there be a hundred? A thousand?

The base seems huge, even from a distance, with lots of smaller outbuildings surrounding a main block. You can see helicopters landing and soldiers running about. As you get nearer you hear alarms going off.

Coming to a massive barbed-wire fence, the Doctor fishes out a slim metal tube. Pointing it at the fence, the device gives off an odd buzzing and the wire uncurls, creating a gap you harmlessly pass through.

'We could've got in over there,' calls Amy, pointing to a part of the fence that is completely shredded. Your stomach tightens – that has to be the werewolves, doesn't it?

It seems the soldiers are too occupied to deal with three trespassers. By the entrance to the main building you see an odd blue box that looks completely out of place.

'Someone knows I'm here,' says the Doctor.

'What?' you ask.

'That blue box. That's my TARDIS. Me and Amy, we travel through time and space in it.'

Just as you're about to say, 'You have got to be kidding,' two soldiers in black uniforms step out of the building with rifles pointing at you.

If you run for it, go to 85.

If you think surrendering is the better idea, then go to 70.

You duck under the Doctor's arm to leave the TARDIS — and straight into the roaring face of a werewolf that's appeared as if from nowhere! The Doctor pushes you out of its way, but the monster swipes at both of you, luckily missing.

Amy cries out, 'Doctor!'

The monster comes towards the Doctor, sniffing at him, then tilts its head as if to look confused. Terrifyingly, it roars into the Doctor's face but then turns and stomps out, further into the monastery, heading towards a bright light.

Amy comes out of the TARDIS. 'I thought you were dead meat, Doctor.'

He turns to you: 'Don't ever, ever do anything like that again. If it hadn't smelt the mistletoe oil on me, we'd have been a dog's dinner.'

You can't apologise enough as the Doctor sprays you and Amy with the mistletoe oil. 'Let's hope this is enough protection — they really don't like this stuff, do they?'

You move towards the room from where the column of bright light reaches into the night sky, seemingly going on forever. You tread carefully, aware that at any moment a werewolf could appear. You've gone past fear now. Your heart has been beating in your chest ever since you saw the werewolf, but your body refuses to let you be scared any more. You're in a daze when you hear a voice crying, 'No, I am

Professor Lazenby! This will not control me. I will control it! It cannot control me!' This is followed by a spine-tingling howl.

If you go towards the voice, go to 15.

If you carry on towards the light, go to 49.

If you have access to a computer, click on box E on screen and enter the code word AWAKE.

If you do not, read on.

You're bundled into the helicopter and the moment you're strapped in, it takes off. The noise from the helicopter engine and the rotor blades is immense. Alongside the pilot is another soldier and they're both dressed in black. Next to you are the man, who you notice is wearing a bow tie, and a woman with long, red hair. They both smile at you.

'I'm the Doctor,' he shouts above the roar of the helicopter's racket. 'This is Amy. Glad you could make it. Sorry about the accident. I tried to get out of the way and so did you and we both got in the way of each other. I clipped your bike, you went flying and you've had a nasty bump. Your bike's a bit of a write-off but it seems you're almost in perfect working order.'

You ask where you're being taken and Amy calls, 'We think this is a military helicopter. The pilot is Captain Jackson and the other soldier is called Eric-something-or-other. It was a bit difficult to hear when they picked us up. It seems they've been chasing the werewolves, too. They want to check us out for infection.'

You tell them that you feel fine and what do they mean by, 'infection'? Before either of them can answer, you all see a huge column of light appear in the distance, reaching straight into the night sky. But it's not in the direction you're heading. You try to get your bearings. The world looks very different from a few hundred feet in the air! You realise the light is coming from the ruins of an old monastery, and tell Amy and the Doctor this.

'If that light doesn't have anything to do with the reappearance of the werewolves then I'm a hungry hexapod.'

The Doctor looks around for something, eventually finding and putting on a headset. As you look towards the light, you're almost certain you can see shadow shapes racing across the countryside towards the ruins, but it could be your imagination running wild.

'Captain Jackson!' the Doctor calls into the headset, 'Head towards the source of the light! If we head to your base it could be too late.' He pauses, listening to the reply which you're oblivious to. You look over to Amy, who is looking at the Doctor and it's obvious she's thinking the same as you – what's going on?

The Doctor puts his hand over the headset mouthpiece. 'The good captain has contacted his base who've agreed we should investigate. Trouble is, they've already got soldiers on the way there.' He looks distant for a moment. 'The last time I faced a werewolf, good people died. We don't know how many of the creatures are on the loose. So, how closely do you think we should land?'

To land as close to the ruins as possible, go to 2.

To land at a distance from the ruins, go to 14.

You decide to lie to the haughty Dr Adams but nervousness takes over. It's no surprise — she is waving a gun in your direction, after all. You tell the scary scientist that the Doctor is investigating the remains of Torchwood House, but you 'um' and 'ah' a little too much and you don't convince Dr Adams at all!

'You think you can fool me? You really are the most dreadful liar. Right, both of you, in front of me, and keep walking. We're off to meet Professor Lazenby. He'll know what to do with you. Don't try anything or someone might get hurt.'

From the direction you're being marched towards, you think you're heading back to the entrance of the base, but you can't quite be sure. You've had an eventful day, after all, it's not over yet, and being held at gunpoint has been one of the easier things to deal with.

Suddenly, the white light of the corridor turns to red and a new alarm starts blaring.

'Oh, no!' exclaims Adams, 'There's a werewolf loose in the building!'

As she says this, thick steel blast doors start to quickly descend from the ceiling. Adams seems to forget about you and Amy as her prisoners, and she races off, her gun at her side, leaving you behind. Obviously the werewolf is more important than two intruders! You hold Amy back for a moment. Staying clear of Adams seems like the best plan you can think of and the werewolf could be up ahead, too.

All the time the blast doors are coming down.

If you let the barrier fall, go to 30.

If not, go to 13.

Taking a deep breath as another spasm of pain tears through your body, trying to hold in the pain and not to shout out, you tell the soldier that you've recently been scratched by a werewolf. Rifles are raised straight away. A dozen safety catches are flicked off. You hold your breath, lean against one of the cold, clammy monastery walls and close your eyes, terrified of what might happen next.

'Gentlemen! Gentlemen!' calls a familiar and reassuring voice. You turn to see the Doctor and Amy rushing towards you. 'You're not thinking of shooting my new friend here, are you?'

'Are all of you infected?' asks the soldier, his weapon raised. You see in the eerie radiance from the pillar of light that he's not the only one. You've never felt so picked on in your life!

'No, just my friend is infected. It was a very, very recent infection, too. And if I can sort out the little problem inside there, there won't be anyone left infected.'

You say, 'I don't feel too good, Doctor.'

'Just hang on. Now, soldier, give me until that light goes out, that's all I'm asking.'

'What are you going to do?'

'Turn it off, stop the werewolves being werewolves and save everyone on this planet. It's what I do. There are dozens of werewolves in there and they're impervious to your bullets. You might want to look that word up. Impervious. Your bullets won't work. But their claws will work on you. Now, come on, you two – left or right?'

'You've got five minutes,' says the soldier. 'Then, impervious or not, we're coming in.'

If you go left, go to 3.

If you go right and have access to a computer, click on box A on screen and enter the code word RUN.

If you go right and do not have access to a computer, go to 83.

You slow your bike as you near the figure. It looks like a large animal in the middle of the road. You stop by a road heading left. In the moonlight the creature looks like some kind of giant wolf! Its breathing is ragged yet hard, steam is coming from its body, its hair is all matted and flat and your imagination is running away with you. Is it covered in blood? Its breath is thick in the cold evening air and suddenly you feel like you should turn tail and get away from the monster. But you're fascinated. You've never seen anything like it – although you're not one hundred per cent certain that you've ever wanted to see something like this.

The monster lifts itself off all fours to stand on its massive hind legs and it howls at the moon. Your stomach clenches, your mouth dries and your heart beats faster. Time seems to have stood still. There is nothing in the world other than the terrifying sound of the creature's howl. You can't quite believe what you're hearing and seeing. The monster is a werewolf! How can that be? They only exist in the movies!

You decide that now isn't the time for thinking. You need to get away from the werewolf. You start pedalling as fast as you can, and race down the road, suspecting the monster with its giant claws and powerful body has got you on its menu for dinner. You look over your shoulder. You're right. The monster has seen you, and you're sure you can see two large cold, blue eyes reflecting in the moonlight.

You have never been so scared in your life. The fear is almost overwhelming and, as you're paying all your attention to the wolf and escaping it, you barely register the sound of a motorbike nearby. At the last second you turn back from the monster to see a motorbike and a sidecar heading straight towards you! You're going to smash right into them!

If you swerve left, go to 12.

If you decide to swerve right, go to 80.

'Smash?' says the Doctor, pointing at the fleshy-crystal platform, 'I'm not even sure I can dent it. I don't know what it is.'

'You need to hurry up and find out,' says Amy. 'Look!'

You both turn to where Amy is pointing. There, hovering in the air, seemingly held by a beam of solid light that's extended from the main column, is a werewolf with a soft glow around its body.

Then there's another, and another, all being picked up from the ground, hanging limply in the air. As you stare you see peculiar purple patterns emerging from the werewolves, and the monsters themselves are becoming more human.

'It's the machine! It's turning them human!' You feel like cheering but your happiness is short-lived.

'I wish I could agree,' says the Doctor. 'I think it's extracting the werewolf element but it needs it. The combination of this number of werewolves and this particular path of the moon passing over the stone – it's no coincidence. The machine's been waiting for tonight for who knows how long.'

'How do we stop it?' asks Amy.

If the machine needs the werewolves, then killing them would stop the machine, you think. And if there was no moon then the machine would stop working, too.

To suggest destroying the remaining werewolves, go to 93.

To suggest stopping the moon, go to 95.

The sound of their footsteps matches your heart pounding in your chest. Suddenly you stick your leg out – and trip Amy instead! The Doctor bursts out and wrestles with the woman, grabs the gun off her and throws it away. Getting up, Amy turns to the woman and punches her – hard! As she falls to the ground, none of you waste any time – you run!

'Now we're all here, we could find out what's going on,' says the Doctor.

'You said we should get out of here!' you say, exasperated at his change of mind.

'Well...'

To find out more, go to 54.

To get out of there, go to 69.

The Doctor digs out a helmet from under the seat and says, 'You are coming, aren't you? I wouldn't feel good about leaving you behind with a werewolf on the loose.' You strap on the helmet good and tight and within moments you're racing across the moor. The journey is bumpy and uncomfortable and you're having to hold on for dear life but after a few minutes you realise you're having an amazing time.

In the cool, moonlit evening, you feel like you could do this forever, until you see shapes moving in the distance, all heading in the same direction. The Doctor slows the bike and stops. Taking off his helmet, he says, 'You can see what they are, yes?'

'More werewolves?' you say.

'I can see about a dozen. This is not good. Not good at all.'

'Why've we stopped?' calls Amy from the sidecar.

'Sorry!' says the Doctor. 'I forget you can't see much down there.' He points to where you can see the creatures race across the distant moor. 'Werewolves. A pack of them.'

'And they're all heading the same way,' you say.

'That's true,' says the Doctor. 'You're a local. What's in that direction?'

'Only the ruins of an old monastery.'

'Of course! We're near St Catherine's Glen. The ruins must be what's left of the Brethren's monastery.'

His words aren't making much sense — you've never heard of 'the Brethren' — but he's right that you're not far from St Catherine's.

'Why would they be going to an old monastery?'

'Good question. Great question. Brilliant question. Perhaps something is calling them? I'm not sure that it matters anyway — there are just too many. I've faced a single lone werewolf before and that caused more than enough problems. I'm not sure I could deal with a pack. I think we need help.'

To suggest the police, go to 4.

To suggest the army, go to 39.

Suddenly a soldier walks in, all battered and bloody. It's obvious he's been attacked by the werewolves! He mutters a feeble, 'Help me...' and collapses onto the cold, hard floor. You see massive claw marks in the back of his black uniform.

'Stay clear,' orders the Doctor and you and Amy step away from the soldier's unconscious body. 'I hate to say it, but this could be just what we need.'

With that puzzling statement he pulls out a syringe and takes a few millilitres of blood from the soldier. He uses his strange screwdriver-device, which buzzes violently for a moment and then stops. The Doctor says, 'I hope there's enough information here to send a counter-signal.'

But at that moment the soldier violently transforms into a werewolf. It's over in a matter of seconds and the monster lunges for the Doctor!

If you have the bottle of perfume, go to 65.

If not, go to 31.

Battling a rising feeling of fear, you follow the Doctor and Amy through the ruins. You see werewolves strolling towards you, but they pass by, ignoring everything around them and, luckily, you!

With the column of light illuminating the countryside, you can clearly see inside the ruins, the broken brickwork, detritus scattered all over the ground, but the massive beam of light casts some very strange shadows. Or is that just your fear again?

'We must follow them,' replies the Doctor. 'The werewolves seem programmed to come here. Why else would they ignore us?'

Just as you step inside, a deep, husky voice rasps at you from the shadows, 'Don't go in there! You'll be torn to pieces!'

You turn to see a figure that's half-human and half-werewolf, but his features shift constantly. Is that an effect caused by the weird light? Every time you see him step out of the shadow he looks different. The fear inside you has risen again. His face looks like he's in so much pain. Sometimes his eyes look human, sometimes they are the bright crystal blue of the werewolves and sometimes the eyeballs are totally black!

'Who are you?' asks the Doctor, reaching forward, not caring about his own safety.

'I was,' comes the growling reply, 'no! I *am* Professor Lazenby.' Just saying this simple sentence has exhausted him as he falls to his knees. 'No! I *will* control it! It will not control me!'

Before your eyes you see him transform into a werewolf, his body growing longer and more powerful, and his face changing shape. The three of you back away but, just as quickly, he becomes more human again.

'It's the Wolf Stone,' he growls, his deep voice cracking with pain. 'It's calling me. It needs me. I'm one of the fifty seeds.'

'Tell me about the stone and the seeds,' says the Doctor urgently, holding Lazenby by his bare shoulders.

'Get back from me!' snarls Lazenby. 'That smell! What is it? What are you carrying?'

'It's mistletoe oil,' explains the Doctor. 'Nothing to worry about.'

'Keep it away from me. The smell, it brings out the wolf.'

'Tell me, how much time do we have?'

'Until the moon reaches its highest point. The stone,' he struggles with the pain as his face starts to change and then reverts back to human. He reaches forward, grabbing the Doctor. 'The stone, it converts moonlight into...something. The wavelength triggers something. A signal, I think. With the fifty seeds, it can spread.'

'What can?'

'Us, me, it. The infection. The parasite. We'll all become monsters. Everyone. I've carried it all my life. I thought I could tame the beast. But the Wolf Stone is calling me. You have to stop it.'

If you have been infected by a werewolf, ask if he knows how to cure it and go to 68.

If not, ask how to stop the signal and go to 25.

Desperately trying to ignore the monster flat out in the middle of the road, you rush over to the crashed motorbike and sidecar by the roadside. The man on the bike is holding his crash-helmeted head, grumbling under his breath words that definitely sound like cursing in a complicated foreign language. He sounds like he's okay, if a bit groggy!

You ask him how he is.

'I'm fine! I'm always fine!' His eyebrows furrow, 'But how's Amy?'

The woman — Amy — in the sidecar pulls off her bright-pink crash helmet, letting down long red hair. She pulls up a pair of airmen's goggles and raises her eyebrows. 'Nothing's broken, Doctor.'

Suddenly, there's an almighty howl and you jump out of your skin! The monster! It roars into the night. You turn around and see the creature marching straight towards you. What do you do?

If you look for a weapon, go to 20.

If you look for an escape, go to 71.

There are dozens of people being held up mid-air by intense beams of light, with swirling purple patterns drifting inside. The patterns float towards the main column. You try to recall which one was picked up first. They're all starting to look the same with the intense glow around their bodies. You're about to decide on one particular man when he suddenly looks down at you and whispers, 'Am... I... free... of... it? Please?'

'Doctor!' you shout. 'Here!'

The Doctor rushes over to you. You see soft waves of a pale-blue light emanating from the stone and dissipate quickly. You're not certain, but you think they're getting stronger.

'No time to gawp,' says the Doctor. 'Give me a bunk-up!'

You knit your fingers together and the Doctor steps onto your hand. 'Now push!' he shouts. You lift him up and straight into the beam of light. Two things happen simultaneously: the Doctor screams and the man he replaced falls to the ground with a bump.

Amy looks terrified. 'You can't do this, Doctor!'

'But isn't the stone looking for stuff that isn't human?' you ask.

'That's right — and the Doctor might have just given his life to save everyone here!'

All you can do is watch, and you're astonished to see a band of golden energy swirling inside the beam being drawn from the Doctor.

From the base of the stone, the waves of blue light are growing stronger and reaching further out before dissipating. You look at the beams. All the figures held by them seem human, without a trace of the werewolf.

When the golden energy strands from the Doctor reach the central column, the whole ground suddenly shakes.

'This is where we find out if his mad plan has worked,' says Amy.

The platform makes a terrible cracking noise. The beams of light shut off and everyone falls to the floor. You race over to the Doctor, who blinks madly at you. 'Ow,' he says simply.

'Are you all right, you, you, you, oh I don't know what you are today!' says Amy.

'Give me a couple of minutes and I'll let you know.'

The huge column of light flickers madly, creating a strobe effect, and then goes out. There's a big explosion as the stone shatters into a million pieces. He did it! The Doctor did it! But what did he do?

'I gave a piece of myself to the machine. The transmitter needed a critical level of haemovariform DNA information to send around the world. I just put my Time Lord biology in the way. But if you,' he says, sitting up and pointing at you, 'hadn't suggested pulling everyone out of the light, I might never have thought of it.'

The only light remaining is the cold luminescence of the moon –

and even that's revealing too much. There are dozens of people in the room and they're all stark naked!

'I think this lot can sort out their own clothing problems,' says the Doctor. 'Don't you? It's probably time we got you home. But would you like a quick trip in my TARDIS first?'

THE END

Quietly, being careful not to be seen by anyone, you call the police, certain they'll help. But they don't believe a word of your whispered story about werewolves and they cut you off, telling you not to mess about with the phone. You can't believe they won't help, but realise how insane you must have sounded.

A shadow passes over your hidden position and you turn to see Lazenby looming over you. 'Trying to call for help, were you? I don't think we'll have any of that,' and he takes the phone from you, and calls over two soldiers. 'Lock these two up in the cage room. They can't be allowed to interfere with the dawn of the Empire of the Wolf.'

'But it won't be an empire, Lazenby, it'll be a slaughterhouse. There'll be carnage. Can you imagine billions of werewolves on Earth all fighting for food? The human population has more than quadrupled in the last hundred years. Billions of carnivores desperate for their next meal. There'll be mass starvation within a year. They'll turn to cannibalism to try to survive. The lupine wavelength haemovariform is a disease – a dead end of evolution.'

'Humanity is the disease, Doctor. Get them out of here!'

If you follow the Doctor's lead, go to 23.

If you fight the soldiers, go to 79.

You go straight on and the three of you race straight into the crumbling monastery. It's all gloomy, forbidding and full of strange shadows cast by the eerie light. You hear the pounding of fast and heavy werewolf footfalls on sodden ground and can't believe that you've made it inside without being eaten alive. You have to stop for breath when you hear gunshots and there's a yelp from one of the monsters.

'Someone out there is on our side,' you say.

'Bullets aren't any good against a werewolf. While the moon is full its body is in a constant state of flux. It forces the human the haemovariform infects to become the monster. If it's powerful enough to do that, a bullet's not strong enough to kill it.'

'Yeah,' you reply, 'but those shots might just have saved our lives.'

'You're right. And we'll use that bit of luck to try to save a few more. Let's find the source of this light.'

'But this place could be crawling with werewolves!' says Amy.

'Then we'll find it carefully.'

The Doctor and Amy go on ahead and you follow. There are things squelching underfoot that you really don't want to think about, and the smell of the place is just rank.

The three of you pass a partially fallen wall and you can see, about a hundred metres away, two soldiers firing at a lone werewolf. Every time there's the crack of a shot, the creature takes half a step back but then surges forward until it's hit by another bullet.

To carry on following the Doctor, go to 3.

To see what happens to the werewolf, go to 24.

You eventually come to a massive control room where a map on a screen dominates the far wall. You realise that it's showing the local area where a large red circle is pulsing, with a white circle pulsing much faster.

You recognise it: 'That's St Catherine's Glen.'

There are a few technicians standing at workstations, operating computers. They all look terrified.

'No one leaves until I say so!' barks a tall, dark-haired man.

The Doctor marches over to him. 'How many werewolves are on the loose?' he demands. 'How long have you people known about this?'

The professor continues working at the console below the screen. The Doctor spies the man's name badge on his white coat. 'From the computer readouts, Professor Lazenby, you've found the exact wavelength to track the werewolves. How did you know that was possible?'

'I know who you are, Doctor. We thought you'd turn up. But you're too late,' says Lazenby, without looking up or answering the Doctor's questions. 'We will contain the werewolves.'

'How long has this operation been going on? Since 1879?'

This makes Lazenby look up. He sees the Doctor for the first time, and there seems to be a flicker of something – is it fear?

'When Queen Victoria was almost infected?' continues the Doctor. 'When the monks of St Catherine's tried to help the werewolf create the Empire of the Wolf?'

'You don't know anything,' says Lazenby, dismissively. 'There was a maid, a cleaner, at Torchwood House. She was cleaning up the blood and the infection passed on.'

'And for more than a century the haemovariform has been growing stronger. Passing it on to so many others. Now there are fifty of the things,' says the Doctor, 'meeting in this area. But how many are there around the world?'

The professor seems to stumble at the Doctor's words and turns to his workstation, saying nothing. He appears to be fighting something. The Doctor looks worried and nods at Amy, who gets out the psychic paper and opens it up. Do you take a look at what it says?

If you take a peek, go to 57.

If you don't, go to 82.

With a pair of tweezers, the Doctor picks up a long, thick silver hair from the road and puts it into a test tube he finds in his jacket. He looks at the hair in the moonlight. 'Really should have put on my leathers for a night like this,' he says, pulling on his jacket. 'It's a bit chilly to be riding around Scotland in winter in tweed. Oh, yes – you asked who we are, didn't you?'

He comes up close to you, and you take an involuntary step back. 'Amy there,' and he points to the woman in the sidecar, 'is from Leadworth. Not the most exciting place in the universe, but you never know where you might find your best friend, do you?'

'What about you?' you ask.

'I'm from a bit further away than Leadworth but, basically, Amy and I travel through time and space, having fun, righting wrongs, saving planets, arguing occasionally but it's mostly about the fun, although everyone focuses on the monsters.'

'You travel through time and space?'

'You've got it. In a brilliantly disguised spaceship. Amy and I are quite good at this sort of thing,' and he vaguely points towards the monster. 'To be honest, Amy's quite new to it. But very useful. Don't tell her I said that, though. I'd never hear the end of it.'

You try to take it all in. The Doctor looks so serious that it's impossible not to believe him, even if what he's saying is crazy. You ask him what he's doing here and he points right back at the werewolf.

'We're chasing that. I thought I'd finished it off about 100 years ago now but it, or its ancestor, or an entirely new breed of creature, has turned up and I really need to sort it out. Are you going to come with us?'

To say, 'If it means risking death by werewolf, then no,' go to 7.

To say, 'I wouldn't miss it!' go to 33.

You tell the Doctor to stop – the Wolf Stone has to extract the DNA from all the werewolves first, or else you'll be left with a very large pack of very hungry werewolves!

The Doctor looks up to see the moon pass into the column of light. As it does so, beams shoot out from the pillar and lift the werewolves, one by one, into mid-air. You can hear a change in pitch every time a beam is fired out. You're amazed at the sight. So many monsters, all lying limply in the rays. It would be almost magical if it weren't quite so terrifying.

'The timing has got to be exactly right for this,' says the Doctor. 'If we get this wrong, it's goodbye Earth and hello Battersea Dogs' Home.'

As the wolf creatures are picked up one by one, the pitch of the sound from the alien transmitter abruptly changes to a deep rumble and you spot a beam of light with no wolf at the end of it. The Wolf Stone keeps on rumbling. On and on it goes. You don't think it's going to work and for a brief second you're ecstatic.

'We're safe!' you cry. 'It's not going to work!'

'No!' shouts the Doctor. 'The haemovariform might live on. More people will get infected.'

'But there's a werewolf missing!' says Amy.

'No,' says the Doctor again. 'There's *someone* missing!'

Time's running out and the moon is about to pass over the column of light. All your efforts will have been for nothing! What are you going to do?

If you've worked out who or what is missing, go to 67.

If you haven't, go to 73.

Taking a look over Amy's shoulder you see that the paper says, 'LAZENBY'S A WEREWOLF.' You're so surprised that you can't help but shout it out. The Doctor and Amy turn to you in horror but everyone else in the room turns to the professor. He turns away from the console with a savage grin. Suddenly the whole of his eyes turn black. There are gasps of astonishment and the scientists in the room back away from him.

'Everyone!' calls the Doctor. 'Out!'

No one needs to be told twice and there's a mad rush for the double doors but you stay behind. You know being with the Doctor is the safest place to be.

In a strange sing-song voice Lazenby says to you, 'Are you sure you don't want to run, child?'

You gulp but don't know what to say to him. The Doctor steps in: 'How can you hold back the transformation, Lazenby? The full moon's been up for hours!'

'My blood sings to me, Doctor,' he replies, 'but I'm the one calling the tunes. Your young friend here,' he says, pointing to you, 'is so very scared. I can see the fear all around. But this one,' he points to Amy, 'she's different, holding back her fear just as I hold back the glory of my transformation.'

'You're staying human by willpower alone?' The Doctor seems

incredulous.

Lazenby smiles a cruel, crooked smile. 'I need to know what your friend's fear smells like.'

His white lab coat doesn't fit so well any more. Dark and silver hair grows from every exposed part of his body. His clothes split and as his hands become paws with curved, deadly claws, he tears them off. His face begins to lengthen, as do his arms and legs. It's all so fast, terrifying and utterly mesmerising. You can barely breathe, never mind move. You're sure that you can hear the sounds of bones cracking and he howls as the change is almost complete.

The Doctor is suddenly in your face, shaking your shoulders. 'We need to move — now!'

The three of you head for the exit but it's barred — by another werewolf!

What do you do? If you run, go to 5.

If you hide, go to 89.

'Sorry for snapping,' says the Doctor, as you both peer at the bizarre structure. Parts of it appear soft to the touch, but you've never seen anything fleshy grow crystals. Just looking at it makes you feel queasy. There seems to be a pulsating light deep within the stone, but you realise that might just be your imagination playing tricks on you.

'What do these crystals do?' you ask.

The Doctor runs his hands through his hair and says with exasperation, 'I haven't a clue! I've piloted Wanarian Star Smashers, defused Aquillian Quantum Bombs that go off if you so much as even look at them, helped to reconfigure a planet's entire ecosystem in minutes but this, this is just so much… mess!'

'Can't the sonic help?' asks Amy.

'It can't even work out what it is.'

Without knowing what you're looking at, you instinctively reach out a hand to touch one of the crystals – but it burns to the touch! You recoil and the Doctor's fascinated by your reaction. He tentatively touches a blue-green crystal and flinches just as you did.

'It burns!' he shouts – then remembers he's in a room full of werewolves and whispers urgently, 'It burns! No! That's not it – *we're* burning *it*!'

Amy asks, 'How come?'

'It's the mistletoe oil. It's not just the werewolves that hate it – it's everything to do with the werewolves!'

With that, he's about to spray the strange edifice with the oil – but someone stops him.

If you stop the Doctor from using the mistletoe oil, go to 56.

If it's Amy, go to 63.

You lie to the soldier and say there's nothing wrong — but at that minute the haemovariform inside you reminds you of its presence. The burning sensation through your blood is worse than ever before. You call out in pain!

'What's wrong with you?' shouts the lead soldier, his rifle raised. You hear a dozen safety catches flicking off.

Your heart is beating so hard in your chest, you feel like it could burst at any second. You're sweating and the pain is incredible. You just want it to stop. Surely the Doctor could make it stop? You try to block out the terrible agony but it's consuming you. You know what's happening — you're becoming a werewolf. You could transform at any second!

Looking at the weapons pointed towards you, you decide to risk it. If anyone can help you, the Doctor can, and if he can't, then at least you tried. But you're not giving up without a fight!

'You have to stay here,' you say, gasping with the pain. 'We don't know how many werewolves are here but we do know — and you know — that your guns don't work. Your weapons are useless. If you follow me, you'll more than likely die!'

You turn and run back towards the light. The soldiers don't follow. You find a room full of werewolves, all lying on the floor around this gargantuan pillar of light that goes on forever. You can see the Doctor and Amy standing in silhouette and you know what they're looking at without having to think about it. It's the Wolf Stone, and it's calling to you. You can hear it singing in the back of your mind. There isn't much time.

You rush towards the Doctor and Amy, to tell them that you can feel the change inside you, but what else do you say?

If you say, 'You've got to turn this off!' go to 35.

If you say, 'We should just smash it to pieces!' go to 94.

The Doctor thinks about your suggestion of pulling the bodies out of the light but Amy spots something unusual. There are strange, purple swirling patterns in the beams of light hitting each werewolf, but the spiralling threads are going towards the central pillar of light.

'What is it?' you ask.

'I've got an idea,' replies the Doctor, 'and you,' he adds, pointing at Amy, 'aren't going to like it, so I'm not telling you what it is.'

He shakes your hand and thanks you for being so brave, and then gives Amy a big hug and thanks her for 'just about everything'. The hug leaves Amy looking worried and confused. 'What are you going to do?'

'Wait and see, wait and see!'

'You're doing that guessing thing again and I don't like it!' Amy shouts, as more of the wolf monsters are lifted up, and the column of light starts to pulse with incredible power.

'I keep telling you – I'm good at guessing! Now, quickly, before this thing reaches critical mass – find the one who looks the most human! And hurry!'

If you find them first, go to 51.

If Amy finds them first, go to 66.

There's something about the woman's manner that puts you off and you try to apologise for being in the restricted area. You say that you and Amy have got lost. But you stumble over your words and it's clear to anyone listening that you're not telling the truth.

Her look of disdain is replaced by one of anger. 'You're obviously intruders. I don't know why you'd want to break into this place, but I intend to find out.'

She fishes a small two-way radio out of her lab coat pocket. 'Security? This is Dr Adams. I'm in the restricted area by the cages. I've two intruders here and need assistance.'

Amy says, 'And these cages, yeah? They're for how many werewolves, exactly? What are you doing with them, Dr Adams? Breeding them? Has it got out of hand yet? With the alarm outside, I'd guess that'd be a "yes". It doesn't matter, anyway. The Doctor's here now. He'll sort them out.'

Suddenly, Dr Adams pulls a small pistol from her other pocket. You instinctively raise your arms but think, 'What sort of scientist carries a gun?'

'The Doctor's here? Where is he? Tell me now!'

If you try to lie, go to 42.

If you tell the truth, go to 26.

You decide the risk is too great and carry on down the road, pedalling faster and faster, knowing that your life depends on escaping the monster on the road behind you. But this is Scotland! You live in a small town almost in the middle of nowhere! Madness like this doesn't happen here. Certainly giant monster wolves don't chase people home after school.

These thoughts are banished from your mind when you hear a roar from the creature. You take a quick, terrified look behind to see the wolf almost on you. You can't pedal any faster, you're going flat out.

You turn again and, for a horrible instant, your eyes are locked upon the wolf's. All you can see in those big blue eyes is rage and hunger. You are its prey and it will devour you. Suddenly, it swipes at your bike. As you go flying over the handlebars, you hear a cry of pain as the creature gets caught up in the bike. Luckily, you land facedown on soft earth by the road. You can't believe you're unharmed — even if you have had the breath knocked out of you.

But it seems your luck has run out. You see the wolf creature leaping over to you. It pins you to the ground with a giant paw. It snarls at you and its teeth are bared. Its breath stinks as it slobbers drool over your face. What do you do?

If you kick out at the monster, go to 71.

If you try to find a weapon, go to 36.

Amy tells the Doctor to stop. At the same time he realises that the Wolf Stone needs to extract the haemovariform DNA from every infected being in the room – or else you'll be left with a room full of monsters!

'And then we destroy the Wolf Stone?' you ask.

'That's if there's enough of the mistletoe oil to do the job,' says the Doctor, holding up the perfume bottle. 'But when slavering werewolves won't go near the stuff, I think there's a good chance that not even half this amount will sort out the Wolf Stone.'

'You're doing that guessing thing again, aren't you?' says Amy.

'I'm good at it!' retorts the Doctor.

You look up into the sky – you can't see the moon! It must have passed into the path of the monumental column of light. All of a sudden, a thinner but just as bright beam shoots out from the light, straight at a werewolf which is lifted into mid-air. More beams shoot out and more monsters are lifted up. They glow in the light. As you watch, hoping that the Doctor's plan to destroy the stone will work, you see that the werewolves are changing, becoming more human. It seems the Wolf Stone is removing all traces of the haemovariform. Just when it appears that all the werewolves have gone, there's a deep rumbling from beneath the Wolf Stone. You notice that there's one beam of light that doesn't have a werewolf at the end of it.

What's going on?

'Is it going to work?' you ask.

'The stone is expecting someone or something else to be at the end of the beam,' says the Doctor.

'But if it doesn't work, the world will be safe, yeah?'

'Well, as safe as it can be with fifty werewolves roaming around, potentially causing havoc across the planet. There's something missing. Can you work out what it is?'

If you can, go to 67.

If not, go to 73.

With the soldiers fighting and the arrival of the werewolf, the Doctor, suddenly serious, decides that you have to get Amy and get out.

'It's just too dangerous around here,' he says. 'I could deal with one werewolf, maybe two or three. But I don't know how many more werewolves are roaming around here.'

The corridors in the base seem endless. There are people rushing about but no one really pays any attention to you, especially not when the base's lights switch from white to red and an alarm starts to sound.

'That can only be trouble,' says the Doctor. 'I wonder if Amy's at the source of it?'

'Surely it'll be more werewolves?' you ask.

The Doctor's about to reply when you reach a junction and stop. You poke your head around the corner — and there's Amy being held at gunpoint by a short woman in a white lab coat!

The Doctor sees this too and tells you to flatten yourself against the wall so the woman with the gun can't see you.

If you decide to wait to push the woman out of the way, go to 91.

If you wait to trip up the woman, go to 46.

Remembering the bottle of perfume, you pull it out of your pocket and squirt it at the wolf. At the same time, the wolf roars into the Doctor's face, as he holds on to its front legs, shouting, 'Help!'

The result is instantaneous! It howls in pain and backs off, flinging the Doctor to one side. He lands in a crumpled heap on the floor.

'Keep squirting it!' Amy cries.

Faster and faster you pump the spray. The werewolf tries to protect itself by covering its head with its front legs. It starts to back away but Amy picks up a metal rod from a table and wallops it around its head, causing the werewolf to collapse.

'Is it dead?' you ask.

As the Doctor picks himself up, there's another massive rumble that shakes the room.

'Dead? I doubt it. They're far too strong. From that tremor, I'd put money on the lupine wavelength signal being imminent,' he says, as he races to a computer and uses the screwdriver thing on it.

'I've encoded the lupine wavelength using the werewolf's DNA. Fed that information into the computer and — you might want to cross your fingers here — set up a cancellation wave.'

'Will it work?' you ask.

'Cross your fingers!'

There's an almighty boom in the distance. 'That's it!' the Doctor cries and presses a single key on the computer. The lights go out! Crossing your fingers hasn't worked!

'Nothing to worry about!' he shouts. 'I'm just using every watt of Scotland's power to create the cancellation wave! There's a blackout across the country.'

A strange white light passes through the air, and is slowly coming towards you when a bright blue light comes the other way and goes right through you. It must be the Doctor's cancellation wave – you're not turning into a werewolf!

Nothing terrible happens to you as the two waves meet. It's as if they're battling one another, with the white light pushing the blue back and vice versa until the blue light suddenly fills the room.

'You did it!' you cry. You see the soldier turned werewolf has become human again – and he's naked!

'We couldn't have done it without you,' Amy says to you.

'If it hadn't been for your quick thinking with the mistletoe oil in the perfume bottle,' adds the Doctor, 'we might have all been dead.'

You all head out of the control room and towards the base's entrance. 'So,' smiles the Doctor, 'it's time you went home – but would you like to go the long way round in the TARDIS?'

THE END

'Uh-oh,' says Amy, pointing at a figure, high off the ground, surrounded by an ethereal glow. 'I think this was the first werewolf.'

And she's right. The man held by the beam is completely human. Any trace of werewolf has been taken from him. He looks at peace, almost happy.

'Oh, no,' says the Doctor, who looks far from happy. 'How am I going to jump up five metres in the air?'

'There's only one thing for it,' you say, but what do you add?

If you say, 'You'll have to destroy the werewolves,' go to 93.

If you say 'You'll have to stop the moon somehow,' go to 95.

If you've guessed anything other than it's you who is the one missing from the beam of light, then you should go to 73.

It's obvious when you realise that the Wolf Stone must be detecting the haemovariform inside you. As soon as you realise, you rush and jump into the beam of light. It's a strange sensation to be held up by nothing but light. Taking a tip from the werewolves all around, you lie as limp as possible in the light.

It's then that you can sense the haemovariform leaving your body. It's a glorious feeling. There's the sensation of being released from a prison that held no chance of escape. Once it's gone, you shout, 'Now, Doctor! Do it now!'

You try to see what he's doing and catch a glimpse of him pouring the oil over the Wolf Stone. The effect is immediate — the rumbling stops, the Stone starts to spark, and Amy and the Doctor have to jump back when a huge cloud of noxious-looking smoke appears. The column of light flickers, the rays holding up all the people who were infected with the haemovariform vanish, and you all tumble to the ground!

You watch the column of light flicker and die. The only light you can see is the baleful light of the full moon. It takes a while for your eyes to adjust — and then you think you're glad you can only see so much, as there are suddenly lots of naked people in the room with you!

You see the Doctor and Amy smiling at you. 'That was very brave,' says the Doctor. 'Anything could've happened to you in that light. I don't always know everything that's going to happen.'

Black-uniformed soldiers enter the room. You hear a shout: 'Everybody stay where you are!'

'I don't think so, do you?' says the Doctor. 'It's time we took you home. Fancy going the scenic route?'

THE END

Lazenby looks at you almost in pity, and shakes his head. 'There's never been any interest in finding a cure,' he says in a low, growling voice. 'Once the moon reaches its zenith, none of this will matter anyway.'

'Why, what happens then?' you ask.

'The Wolf Stone – the source of that light – came with the infection centuries ago. It's been waiting for tonight, growing all these years under the monastery. Now the fifty seeds are here, it will activate fully when the moon falls directly in its path.'

'What does the Wolf Stone do?' demands the Doctor.

'It transmits a carrier wave. Every human being on Earth will transform into a werewolf.'

'Whoa,' says Amy. 'Time to throw a spanner in the works.'

'You're too—' But before Lazenby can finish his sentence his back arches and he screams in pain. The werewolf is taking control once more! Within seconds he's transformed into a ravenous snarling monster. Quickly, you try to back away but the creature swipes at you, breaking the skin on your arm. The pain is intense!

If this is the first time you've been scratched by a werewolf, go to 37.

If this is not your first time and you have access to a computer, click on box A on screen and enter the code word RUN.

If it's not your first time and you do not have access to a computer, go to 83.

As you reach the open ground, you have to take cover when you see black-uniformed soldiers shooting at the werewolves. But their bullets are useless against the creatures and when one of them is hit, it doesn't retaliate... unless the solider is in its path!

'Just how many are there?' you think to yourself. But then you realise that they're – mostly – ignoring the soldiers and are heading in one particular direction, so you tell the Doctor and Amy.

'I noticed that, too,' says the Doctor. 'There must be a reason for it.'

'If we follow them,' says Amy, 'who knows how many we might meet?'

'So we should stay here to find out more?' asks the Doctor.

If you follow the wolves and have access to a computer, click on box C on screen and enter the code word TARDIS.

If you follow the wolves and do not have access to a computer, go to 19.

If you want to find out more, go to 54.

You raise your arms in surrender and Amy follows suit. The soldiers don't look happy and you're not happy about having rifles pointing at your head. The Doctor acts as if the guns aren't even there, however, and demands to know who's in charge, and who thinks they can steal his TARDIS. He walks between the soldiers who follow in his wake until one of them has enough presence of mind to shout, 'Halt!'

The Doctor spins on his heels and smiles at the two soldiers. 'Look, someone here is expecting me. So there's no need for the armed escort. If you can just point the way to whoever is in charge of this... facility, then I can let you go about your jobs protecting the place from the real danger out there. The werewolves, remember?'

With that, he turns back and heads into the main building. The place is absolutely spotless. The walls are so white, they practically shine. You see labs with all sorts of strange equipment, huge offices and meeting rooms. People pass you by and pay no attention to the fact that you're being followed by two armed soldiers.

'Professor Lazenby said we have to escort you to the main control area.'

'That's great. You're doing your job and I'm doing mine.'

'But, erm, sir, the main control area is back the way we came.'

Again, the Doctor turns on his heels. This time you're following the soldiers who eventually lead you to an incredible control room. There are computer banks lining the walls and there are computer screens everywhere, but you haven't a clue what they're showing, except for the massive screen on the far wall that has a map of the local area with lots of red dots pulsing on it, all centring on a faster-pulsing white dot.

'They're tracking the werewolves,' you say.

The man below the screen turns to you, then sees the Doctor and gives a small tight smile. You see the Doctor give Amy a wallet then he strides over to the man and says, 'Professor Lazenby, I presume. Great place you've got here. Ever seen, *You Only Live Twice*? Would you mind telling me what you're doing?'

'You would like that, I'm sure, Doctor,' he says in a deep, gravelly voice. His dislike for the Doctor is obvious, but why? They've only just met!

'You know who I am.'

'We all know.'

You see Amy slowly sneak towards the unguarded exit. What's she doing?

If you decide to follow, go to 81.

If you decide to stay with the Doctor, go to 18.

You look, but there's nowhere to go! You're trapped. The wolf monster has you pinned down, its two giant paws holding you by the shoulders. Its head slowly comes forward towards yours. Its breath stinks. It's dripping thick globules of saliva over you. Its bared teeth are terrifyingly white and sharp. Its breath steams in the cold evening air. You see its fur is matted with dirt and blood. You think this creature from your nightmares is going to be the very last thing you ever see...

Suddenly, the road is lit with two massive spotlights and you hear the rotor blades of two helicopters. You're saved! But who has saved you? The werewolf stands on its hind legs trying to reach for the choppers. Something is fired out of one of them and you see the werewolf bathed in blue light. It howls in agony — it's being electrified. You almost feel sorry for the monster that nearly had you for dinner! You scramble out of the way as it falls to the ground and a weighted net is thrown from the helicopter over the creature.

The man and woman from the motorbike and sidecar reach you, hands raised over their eyes. They blink into the spotlights, as two people in black uniforms and harnesses are lowered to the ground.

'Are you okay?' asks the man, who you notice is wearing a bow tie. Who wears bow ties these days? You nod silently. You're as okay as someone who's just been terrorised by a supposedly mythical creature would be!

As the two people from the helicopter touch down on the road you see the great big guns strapped to their backs. They head straight for the werewolf, ignoring you. That's some fearsome-looking weaponry and is nearly as terrifying as the monster that was about to eat you. The night has gone completely crazy and is getting crazier. You've got the perfect chance to get away. Do you take it?

To get out of this madness, go to 7.

If you want to find out more and have access to a computer, click on box E on screen and enter the code word AWAKE.

If you want to find out more, but don't have access to a computer, go to 41.

You look around the room – or what's left of it. One wall had collapsed at some point in the past, so that it's exposed to the outside world. Could there be some clue here that would stop the transmitter sending its signal to turn everyone in the world into werewolves?

You stare at the vast column of light, noting that there are swirling patterns within it. Your eyes travel over the werewolves, all lying prostrate on the ground, circling the light and the stone, as if praying to it. The Doctor walks around the stone, and even in the column's strange radiance you can see he's desperate for an answer – and none is forthcoming.

Threading a path through the entranced werewolves, you hear a sudden deep chime emanating from the stone.

'What was that?' you call back.

'I don't think it was the dinner gong,' says the Doctor.

A beam shoots out from the pillar of light, a fierce and powerful ray that lifts a werewolf from the ground, somehow making the monster glow at the same time. Then another. And another. Then you're lifted off the ground too!

You can feel the haemovariform leaving you – it's all going to be all right, you think. The infection is being taken from you. The Doctor's got it wrong. The stone is here to cure the werewolves, not make more of them!

You see the Doctor frantically working at the stone. Sparks come off it but soon all the werewolves in the room are being held in mid-air by the light beams and it seems nothing the Doctor can do will stop it.

The light cuts out and you fall to the ground with a thump. Is it over? Maybe not – there's a strange noise coming from the stone...

'We're missing a piece of the puzzle!' shouts the Doctor. 'I can't stop the signal! Quickly! Both of you! I can use the sonic screwdriver to protect us!'

You and Amy race to reach the Doctor's side as he holds up the screwdriver that causes the air around it to ripple a shimmering red. You see Amy is safe but then an enormous wave of light bursts from the stone. You haven't reached the Doctor in time. You can feel your body changing, becoming stronger, taller, and hungrier! You see two people before you, their mouths open wide in shock.

'Back to the TARDIS,' says the man. 'Hopefully we can reverse the process from there.'

But all you can feel is the haemovariform inside your mind screaming, 'Victory! At last – the Empire of the Wolf is born!'

THE END

The Doctor shouts, 'It's you, of course!'

Suddenly understanding, you rush and jump into the beam of light. Floating in mid-air is a strange experience and, from the looks on Amy and the Doctor's faces, you're not completely certain that this is going to work. When you feel the haemovariform being extracted from your body, your confidence grows and you begin to enjoy the sensation. And you just might be helping to save the world!

All at once you feel human again and the room resonates with a deep chime. The column of light becomes almost blinding but, silhouetted, you can see the Doctor pouring the oil onto the stone. Its effect is immediate! You can hear vicious hissing and popping – the oil must be acting like some sort of acid – and a huge cloud of smoke erupts over the Wolf Stone, making the Doctor and Amy cough and splutter.

The column of light flickers, and the beams extending from it go out rapidly, one by one, and you and everyone else who'd been infected by the haemovariform fall to the floor. The vast pillar of light is extinguished and you're plunged into almost total darkness. It takes a moment for your eyes to adjust to the gloom as the only light you have now is from the distant moon.

You hear a distant voice say, 'Men, surround the area and round up everyone you can find.'

'Come on, you,' says the Doctor, helping you to your feet. 'Let's scarper before those soldiers get here.'

'We did it?' you ask.

'We definitely did,' he replies. 'And if you hadn't been here, who knows what might have happened. Come on, it's time to take you home. Do you remember where you parked your bike? I wonder if it's still there…'

THE END

The Doctor shouts as you run towards the motorbike: 'There's a helmet under the seat!' Fumbling with the seat, you hear the scrape of the werewolf's claws on the road. You try to concentrate as you put on the helmet, but you're all fingers and thumbs and it's taking forever!

The Doctor jumps onto the bike, checks on Amy who shouts out, 'This werewolf hunt is going well, isn't it? Except the werewolf is now hunting us. You told me that wouldn't happen.'

The Doctor steers the bike and its sidecar down the road. You look back to your bike — at least on the motorbike you'll get away from the werewolf. You realise an abandoned bike isn't that important. There's a monster on the loose!

With the bike roaring down the road, you call out to the Doctor, asking if he does this all the time. 'Pretty much,' he shouts back. 'People, planets, petunias, the lot. There's usually lots of running too. But you can't outrun a werewolf for long. I'm glad I found the Royal Enfield parked up in the TARDIS. Many a bank holiday spent down in Brighton. Good times.'

You ask the Doctor what a TARDIS is.

'That's my ship.'

'Ship?' you repeat.

'Yep, ship. With it I can travel anywhere in time and space.'

That seems crazier than the werewolf! There's a part of you that thinks you should be heading home but this is too exciting. You ask about the werewolf. Isn't it dangerous out there on the moors? The Doctor agrees.

'There aren't many people about though, and it hasn't followed us. I need to find out where it's from before I can deal with it.'

'Shouldn't we call the police?'

The Doctor slows the bike to a stop by a tall, dark-blue box, a sign states that it's a 'police public call box'. You're confused as to what's going on, as Amy steps out of the sidecar and the Doctor jumps off the bike. He fishes out a key and asks, 'Are you coming?'

'Are we phoning the police?'

Amy smiles. 'Better than that.' And she follows the Doctor who's used the key to open the box and stepped inside.

You follow, and what you see astounds you. Contained within the blue box – the TARDIS – is another room entirely, with a high ceiling and stairways. Dominating the space is a many-sided contraption with all manner of levers, dials, buttons and meters over it. Everything on it seems recognisable but you can't understand any of it. Most impressive is the glass pillar that fits into the machine, coming from the ceiling.

As you recover from the shock, the Doctor, standing at an old-looking screen shouts, 'A-ha! I knew it! Lupine wavelength haemovariform DNA! Now, is it descended from the one I met in 1879 or is it a recent arrival?'

He races about, pressing buttons, checking instruments. 'That's not right. Worse, that's not good.'

You and Amy exchange glances.

'There are, yes, that's right, there are fifty werewolves in the area. Fifty!'

'We can deal with that, yep?' asks Amy.

The Doctor pulls a face. 'We've got two choices. There are just a couple over here,' he says, pointing to the screen, 'and a few on the move, heading towards what must be a pack of werewolves.'

If you investigate 'a couple' of werewolves, go to 9.

If you want to investigate the pack and you have access to a computer, click on box C on screen and enter the code word TARDIS.

If you want to investigate the pack and do not have access to a computer, go to 19.

The narrow alley is only just wide enough for your bike. You lightly clip the handlebars on the stone walls on either side, but you don't care about the damage you might be doing to your bike. You care about the damage the monster behind you could do to you! With expert skill, you barely slow the bike's speed as you hurtle down the alley. The only thought in your head is to escape from the wolf. You hear a roar behind you but you daren't turn round – it'd be too dangerous to do so in such a tight space. You just keep hoping that you've done enough to be free of the creature.

It feels like it takes forever to reach the end of the alleyway and get onto a main road. You bump down a few steps from the alley. You risk a look over your shoulder: there's no one and nothing coming after you. Brilliant! You've escaped the monster! You look around you and try to get your bearings. Where exactly are you?

It doesn't take long to reach home, however, and you don't feel like you can tell anyone there what's happened to you. Would they believe you? Later in the evening as you're sat watching TV in your room, you start to wonder if what you saw was real. And who were the people on the motorbike and sidecar? Why would they be chasing the wolf creature? Perhaps it had escaped from a zoo? As these thoughts and a thousand more cross your mind, an unearthly white light passes through your room. You suddenly feel sick and in tremendous pain!

The room starts to spin as you fall to the floor. The last thing you know is that you're changing, growing taller and hairier, with claws extending from powerful hands. Everything is blurry with confusion and pain. The thought 'Why is this happening?' is your very last as suddenly your mind is not your own any more...

THE END

Lazenby barks a short, sharp laugh. 'It's only my willpower keeping me from turning into a wolf. But the Stone is calling me to it. It needs me. And the moon is so high tonight. It makes my blood sing.'

A shiver passes down your spine. You think you understand how he feels. But the feeling that's racing around your body is nothing like singing. You feel as if your body is on fire.

'Stay with us!' commands the Doctor, holding your body up as it starts to go limp. The wolf inside you is desperate for release.

'You've got to hold on!' cries Amy desperately.

'We will find an answer to this,' adds the Doctor. 'And we've only just met. You can't go anywhere yet!'

You try to smile and focus, but you're feeling nauseous. The room is spinning around you and you can't make out people's features. The wolf is winning! Suddenly your body is wracked with pain and you scream as your back arches – you're changing shape! You're changing species!

Your body grows longer and more powerful and you can see your hands turning into paws with strong, yellowing claws growing out from them. You're losing control of yourself as you turn into a monster! Your last thought before the transformation is complete is that you hope you don't harm the Doctor and Amy, but now you'll never know – you're a werewolf!

THE END

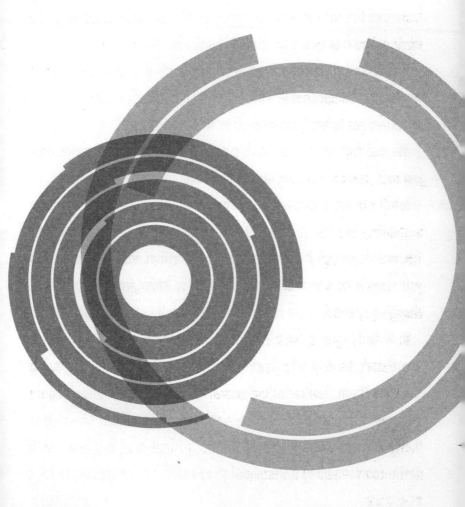

'Let me think, let me think,' says the Doctor, pacing up and down in front of the huge monitor. 'More than nine centuries old – I'm sure the synapses are slowing down. But I've not been in this body that long. I should be firing on all cylinders!'

And then he turns and stares at you and you can't help but stare back at those deep eyes. Neither of you are blinking.

'I marched in here,' he begins, 'acting as if I owned the place. There were seven people working at their computers, Lazenby stood more or less where I'm standing now. No one is smiling. Two people look exceptionally scared. The alarm is blaring. Someone asks in a nervous voice if it can be turned off. Lazenby doesn't turn round. He doesn't answer. He doesn't say anything. He's staring at the screen. He looks scared and eager at the same time. What's so important about the screen? There's a series of red pulses and there's a white one, too. What's that white pulse for? We know what the red is... there's a number, no, a timer in the corner. It's counting down. I tell him that he's got to stop. We have the usual argument about who the blazes am I. All the boring stuff. Done it too many times. But Lazenby is still working at the computer. And the white pulse and the countdown vanish.'

'What does it mean?' you ask.

'There's something in the monastery ruins, an energy source for a signal of some kind, at a guess.'

'What will it do?' asks Amy.

'No idea,' says the Doctor, working at the computer. 'But I can guess that it won't be good.' His fingers blur over keyboards around him. He dashes from one console to another, returning to the one under the screen. Within a minute you see a countdown and a white pulse on the screen.

'And what about the countdown?'

'I think we've got about twenty minutes to save the world. Been there and done that a few times, too. That never gets boring. It is a signal. There's something at the monastery that will transmit the lupine wavelength around the world.'

You suddenly realise what this means, 'So—'

'Yes,' interrupts the Doctor, 'in about twenty minutes every human on Earth will be a werewolf!'

If you head for the source of the signal and have access to a computer, click on box C on screen and enter the code word TARDIS.

If you head for the source of the signal, but do not have access to a computer, go to 19.

If you want to try to block it from the control room, go to 48. Remember, time is running out!

The Doctor turns the motorbike around and you head back the way you came. You're not really sure where you're going but you trust this Doctor for some reason, despite the fact that you've only just met him. If it wasn't for Amy though, you'd think the Doctor was a bit mad.

'This werewolf hunt is going well, isn't it?' shouts Amy. 'We were looking for one and we've found a dozen!'

The Doctor's brow furrows but he ignores her and steers the bike and its sidecar back down the road.

With the bike roaring down the road and the wind rushing past you, you call out to the Doctor, asking if he does this kind of thing all the time. 'Pretty much, yep,' he shouts back. 'I've fought alien tortoises, megalomaniacal seaweed, killer robots, the lot. Anyway, there's lots of running.' He pats the bike. 'So I'm glad I found the Royal Enfield parked up in the TARDIS. Many a bank holiday spent down in Brighton.'

You ask, 'What's a TARDIS?'

'That's my ship. Me and Amy, we can travel anywhere in time and space.'

You don't believe him but say nothing as you race on. There's a part of you that knows you should be heading home but you distract those thoughts by asking about the werewolves. Aren't they dangerous on the loose? The Doctor agrees. 'But I think I can count the number of people on the moors on a chilly November evening on no fingers.'

The Doctor slows the bike to a stop in front of a tall, dark blue box. Amy steps out of the sidecar and the Doctor slides off the bike, swinging one leg over the handlebars. He fishes out a key and asks, 'Are you coming in?'

'Are we phoning the police?' you ask, noting the sign above the door.

Amy smiles. 'Better than that. Much, much better than that.' And she follows the Doctor in.

Nervous and excited, what you see takes your breath away. Inside the box — the TARDIS — is another room, with a high ceiling and stairways. Dominating the space is a six-sided alien-looking workstation — an engine? — with levers, dials, buttons and meters. Most impressive is the glass pillar that fits into the machine's centre, coming from the ceiling. There's a constant thrum of power and you're in awe of it.

The Doctor, standing at an old-looking screen shouts, 'A-ha! I knew it! Lupine wavelength haemovariform DNA! Now is it descended from the one I met in 1879 or is it a recent arrival?'

He races about, checking instruments on the layouts around him. 'You know that dozen werewolves?'

You and Amy exchange glances and you simultaneously say, 'Yes...?'

'Try about fifty.'

'We can deal with that, yep?' asks Amy.

The Doctor pulls a face, like he's not so sure. 'We've two choices. There are just a couple over here,' he says, pointing to the screen, 'and a few on the move, heading towards what must be a pack of werewolves, here.'

If you decide that you should investigate just the 'couple' of werewolves, go to 9.

If you want to investigate the pack, and have access to a computer, click on box C on screen and enter the code word TARDIS.

If you want to investigate the pack and do not have access to a computer, go to 19.

You prepare yourself to leap at the soldiers but all they have to do is point their guns and everyone stops.

'There's a fine line between bravery and stupidity,' the Doctor tells you, gently. 'A superior force isn't beaten by using force in return. It's defeated by something else entirely.'

'What?'

The Doctor just taps the side of his head.

'Get them locked up in the cage room,' orders Lazenby. 'I don't want to see them again tonight. And when the signal comes, I want them to be tormented in their prisons until they starve!'

The soldiers bundle you out of the room and the Doctor tries to start up a conversation, asking about family and friends. It's obvious he's trying to make the soldiers think about their situation, the job they're doing and the consequences of what Lazenby is planning.

But the soldiers refuse to speak and every time the Doctor stops and turns to them he's pushed roughly onwards.

The lights suddenly falter and the glaring white light along the corridors is replaced by red emergency lighting. You, the Doctor and the soldiers stop as an alarm blares out.

'Someone in dire need of a disco?' mutters the Doctor, almost to himself.

Then you see the reason for the alarm — a werewolf! You're

confused when the soldiers start shooting. Didn't the Doctor say the Brethren worshipped the wolf?

'Bullets won't work against it!' shouts the Doctor, grabbing you by the arm and running back the way you came. 'You need to run!'

You take a quick left then turn right, then down another left, running all the time, and hear the sounds of gunshots cease, replaced by two short-lived screams. You pass a room and hear Amy shout, 'Doctor!' And you find her in a room full of tall, tough-looking metal cages. The Doctor uses a device that buzzes at the cage's electronic lock, causing it to spark and the cage door to open.

'Things are getting a bit desperate here,' the Doctor tells Amy. 'We've met Lazenby, leader of a werewolf cult, and he knows why the werewolves are gathering at the ruins of a monastery not too far from here. Now there's a werewolf loose in the base, too. It seems whatever Lazenby has been planning for the creatures isn't working out. Do we risk getting locked up again by getting more information from Lazenby, or do we fly blind into the lair of the monsters?'

To talk to Lazenby, go to 87.

To follow the werewolves, go to 69.

It's very strange, but suddenly you come to in a helicopter – which is in the air! You've been unconscious! The noise from the helicopter engine and the rotor blades is immense. And it's freezing! There's a door open which is letting a constant blast of wind chill you to the bone. Alongside the pilot is another soldier. They're both dressed in black uniforms. Behind them and next to you are an odd-looking man and a woman with long, red hair. They both smile.

'I'm the Doctor,' he shouts above the roar of the helicopter's racket. 'This is Amy. Glad you could make it. Sorry about the accident. I tried to get out of the way, so did you and we both got in the way of each other. I clipped your bike, you went flying and you've had a nasty bump. Your bike's a bit of a write-off but it seems you're almost in perfect working order.'

He nods towards your head and you carefully pat your forehead where you discover a tender bump that feels like it's the size of a small country!

You ask where you're being taken and Amy calls, 'We think this is a military helicopter. The pilot is Captain Jackson and the other one is called Eric-something-or-other. It was too difficult to hear when they picked us up. They've been chasing the wolf creature – but there's more than one of them. They want to check us for infection and to check your head. You've been out cold for a good ten minutes.'

You say you feel fine and what do they mean, 'infection'? Before either answers you all see a huge column of light appear in the distance, reaching into the sky. But it's not in the direction you're heading. You try to get your bearings. The world looks very different from a few hundred feet in the air. You work out the line is coming from the ruins of an old monastery, and you tell the Doctor this.

'If that light doesn't have anything to do with the reappearance of the werewolves then I'm a chocolate-iced and custard-filled doughnut with sprinkles.'

The Doctor looks around for something, eventually picking up a headset. As you look out towards the light, you think you can see shadowy shapes racing across the countryside towards the monastery ruins.

'Captain Jackson!' the Doctor bellows into the headset. 'Head towards the light! If we head to your base we could be too late.' He pauses a minute, listening to the reply. You look over to Amy and it's obvious she's thinking the same as you: what's going on?

The Doctor puts his hand over the headset's mouth piece. 'The captain's contacted his base who've agreed we should investigate. Trouble is, they've already got soldiers on the way there.' He looks distant for a moment. 'The last time I faced a werewolf, good people died. We don't know how many of the creatures are on the loose. So, how closely do you think we should land?'

To land as close to the ruins as possible, go to 2.

To land at a distance from the ruins, go to 14.

Avoiding the soldiers criss-crossing the base is surprisingly easy. Everyone seems to be more concerned with what might be causing the alarm than with anything or anyone else. And when you and Amy do get odd looks she flashes the wallet at them and they seem happy with what they've seen.

'The Doctor calls it psychic paper,' says Amy, looking at your puzzled face as she waves the wallet once more. 'It's supposed to tell people what I want them to think. It can save us a lot of time but, like everything else with the Doctor, you can't rely on it totally.'

You come to a door at the side of the massive warehouse. It isn't locked.

Inside is a long corridor that's coloured a drab, institutional grey and seems to go on forever, lit by harsh fluorescent light-strips from a low ceiling. There doesn't seem to be anyone around. You can hear the gentle hum of air conditioning that's keeping the place cool, but the air smells stale.

'Don't sneak about,' orders Amy, 'otherwise people might just guess that we're not supposed to be in here.'

'But we're not supposed to be in here, are we? And what are we looking for?'

'We're looking for anything out of the ordinary. Anything that might tie in with the lone werewolf that the Doctor saw was around here. Just pray we don't meet the werewolf.'

You carry on walking along the corridor. There are windows into other rooms, labs with scientific equipment and computers everywhere.

'How will the Doctor deal with the werewolves?' you ask.

'I don't know, but I'm sure he's dealt with worse. He said he'd met one around here at a place called Torchwood House. Do you know where that is?'

You've never heard of it and say so.

'From what the Doctor told me, there was this group of monks who tried to use a werewolf to infect Queen Victoria and make her a werewolf and so take over the British Empire.'

'But Queen Victoria died in 1901!'

'Time machine, remember? Anyway, these monks had tried to trap Victoria at Torchwood House but the Doctor found out the house itself was a trap for the werewolf. All very clever, apparently.'

'There are ruins of a monastery not that far from where I live,' you say.

'Really? I bet the Doctor will want to know that.'

You and Amy reach two massive metal doors that are locked with a card reader. Amy fishes out a metal card and opens the doors.

'Where did you get that from?' you ask.

'Don't tell the Doctor,' says Amy. 'He keeps telling me off for picking pockets!'

As the doors slowly slide into the wall, you see a huge room filled with tall, thick-barred steel cages. You realise that you don't need to be Einstein to work out what should be in the cages.

'Excuse me,' says a snooty voice behind you. 'Just who are you and what are you doing in this restricted area?'

You both turn to see a short, sharp-featured woman in a white lab coat, with dark hair and the hint of a sneer on her face.

If you decide to let Amy do the talking, go to 21.

If you want to do the talking, go to 61.

Just as you decide not to look, a werewolf bursts into the room and, incredibly, Professor Lazenby turns into one too!

The transformation is as astonishing as it is fast. One second there's a man standing by the computer, the next there's the sound of clothes tearing, as a three-metre-tall wolf monster bursts through them, roaring into the air as he does so. Everyone is transfixed by the change until someone screams and then you realise you must run or hide!

If you run, go to 5.

If you hide, go to 89.

**If you have access to a computer, click on box A on screen
and enter the code word RUN.**

If you do not, read on.

The three of you race towards the source of the light and come
to a room that's exposed to the outside world; two of its walls have
collapsed and there's no roof. The column of light that reaches into
space dominates everything and is so bright that it bleaches all
colour – everything is in monochrome. Around the strange pillar
are dozens of werewolves, all lying flat. There's an abrupt pulse
from the column and the light grows more intense. In unison, the
werewolves howl – and there's a part of you that wants to join in!
How much longer do you have before the change happens?

The Doctor carefully wends his way towards the light, stepping over
the monsters that, incredibly, ignore him. The werewolves seem to be
in some kind of trance.

You and Amy look at each other, take deep breaths and follow
him. Reaching the base of the strange light, you see that a huge kind
of stone has recently been pushed through the ground. You can see
fresh earth that has been displaced as the strange boulder rose up.

This is the Wolf Stone. It looks like grey-green flesh with multi-
coloured crystals growing in to the flesh and protruding from it. You
don't know what to make of it. You just know that it's alien. There's

nothing on Earth like this. It just looks wrong.

If you ask the Doctor, 'Is there an off switch?' go to 35.

If you ask, 'Can you smash it to pieces?' go to 94.

Keeping the device pointed at the monster is causing it incredible pain and you can barely think or breathe because the noise is so intense, but you're determined that the creature shouldn't harm you or the people on the bike. Suddenly it leaps up on all fours and, with a last malevolent look behind at you with piercing blue eyes full of rage, it bounds off into the distance over a field, heading for the moors.

When you feel sure the monster has gone, you take your finger off the button and the silence is possibly the best thing you have ever heard. Your head is pounding and your heart is thumping in your chest as the man comes over and shakes you by the hand. 'I'm the Doctor, and this,' he says, pointing to the woman who's taken off her bright-pink crash helmet, 'is Amy. What you did was very brave. Standing up to a werewolf. Wow. Thank you.'

You feel a bit shaky from all the adrenaline rushing around your body but ask, 'Was that really a werewolf?'

'Absolutely. And we need to get after it. Come on, Pond,' he calls to Amy, 'let's get the bike out of there and head off.'

He turns back to you and then over to where the werewolf vanished into the distance. 'Do you know what's out there?'

'Some old ruins,' you say. 'Meant to be an old monastery. Our school visits every now and again.'

'Your school visits the monastery of the Brethren? Of the Cult of the Wolf?'

'The what?'

'This cult that liked werewolves. One in particular, anyway. Liked it a lot. Worshipped it. Didn't quite realise that it was an alien parasite. Wanted to infect Queen Victoria and take over the British Empire.' He smiles at you. 'I stopped them of course, otherwise round here would be a very different place. So, St Catherine's Glen is that way, then?'

You try to take in everything he's said and two questions form in your mind.

To ask if they should contact the police, go to 4.

To ask who Amy and the Doctor really are, go to 55.

You make a mad dash for freedom. You hear a cry of 'Halt!' and a shot is fired over your head. This doesn't stop you – it spurs you on! You hurtle around the side of the base, ignoring the pain in your lungs and the pounding of your heart in your chest. You come to a stop by a door marked 'Emergency Exit' and realise Amy is right behind you! She takes the wallet the Doctor had given to her, uses to it swipe through an electronic card reader and the door hisses open.

'Get in!'

You don't need telling twice. Diving inside, you wonder what sort of trouble you're going to land in now.

'What about the Doctor?'

'I guess he was captured. It's quite a serious occupational hazard.' She sees you looking worried. 'Believe me – he'll be fine. He's the Doctor.' She takes a look around. 'Oh, lovely. Corridors. My favourite.'

And she's right, you're marching down one gleaming, brightly lit corridor after another. If you weren't so nervous of bumping into any more soldiers, or worse, werewolves, then you might think this was a bit dull! The tedium is broken when you come to a vast room full of cages. All of them have thick, strong metal bars, electronically locked, and all of them, you're happy to see, are empty. You know what these are for – the werewolves. What are they doing in this place?

As you both wander around the 'cage room' you hear a polite

coughing from behind you. There, by the door, is a short woman with sharp, mean features and dark hair. She looks as if she's forgotten how to smile.

'Who are you, please?' she asks, pleasantly, but there's a coldness in her voice and you're not fooled by her politeness for a second. She knows what's supposed to be kept in here. She knows about the werewolves too.

If you try to be equally polite and then leave, go to 61.

If you let Amy do the talking, go to 21.

From your hiding place you call home and the phone rings and rings without answer. You feel as if everyone in the room can hear the ringing tone but know that the sound of Lazenby and the Doctor's arguing is drowning out every sound in the room. The call redirects to the messaging service and you try ringing again. There has to be someone there! There must!

Then the tone cuts out, emergency red lighting fills the room and an alarm starts blaring out. Risking a look over the edge of the workstation, you see a werewolf in the doorway. The Doctor quickly hides while Professor Lazenby clutches his head in his hands. Surely, he can't be…? You watch in fascination as hair grows from his hands, which transform into powerful claws on strong front legs. His changing form fills his clothes until they split. He moves his paws away from his face. Professor Lazenby is now a werewolf!

But the figure that was once Lazenby seems dazed by the transformation. The creature is unsteady on its feet and it lets out a small yowl of pain. What's wrong with it? The werewolf by the doorway steps inside, seemingly puzzled by the beast that was Lazenby.

This could be a perfect time to flee both monsters, you decide.

If you run, go to 5.

If you stay hidden, go to 89.

The control room is eerily deserted. There are no lab technicians standing at computer workstations. All the computers have been powered down. The large screen that dominates the far side of the room is blank. The emergency red lighting throws a sombre shade over everything and only the distant sound of gunfire reminds you that there is life on the base. Could a werewolf walk into the room at any moment?

'There's no one here,' you say. 'We should be following the werewolves, shouldn't we?'

But the Doctor is staring at the large dead computer screen. 'I feel like I've forgotten something, but what?' he asks no one in particular.

Amy tugs his elbow. 'Doctor, we'll find out nothing here. Let's go. Frankly, this place is beginning to get on my nerves.'

The Doctor turns and smiles. 'You're right. Absolutely right.' He starts to march out of the control room. 'Come on, Pond!' But then he stops and turns back.

'It's just I've got this feeling, like it's someone's birthday and I know it is and I've got them a present and arranged a party but I've forgotten whose birthday it is. Or it's like waking up from a brilliant dream but not remembering a single detail about it. Everyone's had that, haven't they?'

'Come on, Doctor. Let's get after the werewolves.' Amy stops.

'I never thought I'd ever say anything like that.'

If you think the Doctor should investigate further, go to 77.

To go after the werewolves in the TARDIS and if you have access to a computer, click on box C on screen and enter the code word TARDIS.

If you want to go after the werewolves and you do not have access to a computer, go to 19.

You dash straight into the monastery ruins. There's nothing like three-metre-tall werewolves to get the adrenaline pumping and the legs racing. You didn't know you could run so fast. As soon as you're inside you realise that you're not being followed by the monstrous werewolves. You're puzzled but very glad.

Leaning against a wall to get your breath back, you discover that it's clammy to the touch – the place is falling apart. The smell of damp brickwork and decay fills your nostrils. The monastery roof seems to have collapsed decades ago; bricks and roof tiles line the floor, and most of the monastery is open to the sky. You suddenly feel absolutely freezing and are a bit freaked out by the vast column of light making creepy shadows on the walls.

'I'm sure I don't need to say this to either of you,' says the Doctor, 'but let's be very, very careful.'

'We're walking into the werewolf lair,' says Amy, as if she's realising for the first time just what she's doing.

'You could've stayed in Leadworth,' replies the Doctor lightly.

'You wish.'

'Come on, you two,' you say. 'Keep it down. We don't want to disturb anything, do we?'

Walking down all that remains of a long hall, keeping to the walls and in the shadows wherever possible, you hear a voice muttering nearby. You all stop in your tracks and strain to listen.

'I am not a monster. I am not a monster,' comes the desperate exclamation. 'I am Professor Lazenby! I am not a monster! I will control it! It will not control me!' But this is followed by a dreadful, pained howl that sends shivers down your spine.

From the man's voice it's obvious he needs help. But you also know that you don't have much time and need to investigate the source of the light.

If you follow the voice, go to 15.

If you decide to follow the light, go to 49.

You hide behind a bank of computers and you can hear shouts, gunshots, roars and howls — but you can't see Amy or the Doctor! The gunshots suddenly stop and as you slowly try to peer over the computers you can't see anyone or anything but the werewolves — who howl once more. You're also desperate to know if Amy and the Doctor are okay. What do you do?

If you stay hidden, go to 11.

If you try to find Amy and the Doctor and you have access to a computer, click on box B on screen and enter the code word NOW.

If you try to find Amy and the Doctor and do not have access to a computer, go to 16.

You look at the werewolves pacing near the TARDIS. It's almost as if they're waiting for something. Or maybe they're just hungry and can smell human flesh in the air!

'We can't wait here hoping they'll head off at any minute,' says the Doctor. 'We'll have to head for the helicopter. Come on!'

As you and Amy run after him and race across the base, it gives you a moment to think about what's happening. You can't believe that you're going to steal a helicopter from a military base, but from what you've learnt so far, a stolen chopper is going to be the least of people's problems if you, Amy and the Doctor don't find out what's going on with the werewolves.

At any moment you're expecting a soldier to stop you or a werewolf to leap out and attack you. You're sensitive to everything around you and suddenly feel incredibly alive. When you reach the helicopter, you still expect to be shot at, but the Doctor gets everyone strapped in and starts the engine – which splutters and dies.

'You can fly one of these things, Doctor?' asks Amy.

'Primitive Level Five technology like this? You have got to be kidding, right?'

After a couple more false starts, the helicopter rotor is at full blast. Shakily, the Doctor gets the vehicle into the air. You're shocked to see an incredible beam of light shoot up into the night sky. You can't work out how wide it is, but it seems to go on forever.

'I think that was a definite clue,' says the Doctor over the noise of the helicopter.

Within moments you're coming towards it. Everything looks kind of strange in the spooky radiance given out by the column of light, but when you see a dilapidated and abandoned building, you know just where you are.

'We're near the monastery ruins in St Catherine's Glen,' you say.

'Can you see the werewolves heading towards it?' asks the Doctor. 'Who knows how many there are?'

As you peer towards the ground you think you can just about see shadowy shapes racing to the monastery.

'We should land,' says the Doctor. 'But how close?'

If you think you should land as close to the ruins as possible, go to 2.

If you want to land at a fair distance, go to 14.

As the woman and Amy pass the junction, you take a deep breath and dive for her legs, but you trip them both up! As legs and bodies become confused, the Doctor reaches over to the woman and grabs the gun from her hand and throws it down the corridor.

'Right,' he says, 'you carry a gun so already I don't like you. That you've been pointing it at my friend here makes me like you even less. And I try to like everyone, don't I, Amy?'

'Just who are you?' asks the woman.

'That's not important, is it? The rampaging werewolves outside most definitely are.' He leans into the woman's face. 'And you've got answers, haven't you?'

The woman stares back at him, her eyes full of anger.

'She's Dr Rachel Adams,' says Amy when the woman refuses to speak. 'I met her coming through the emergency exit at the side. They've got these monumental cages for you-know-what back there.'

'The werewolves are your fault? You've been deliberately creating werewolves? Are you monumentally stupid? That's got to be like playing with fire while being in the frying pan.'

Dr Adams rolls her eyes, as if she's heard the argument before. 'You really don't know anything. Professor Lazenby will have this all under control before the morning. The subjects are reacting to something up by the old monastery. We can find out tomorrow.'

'Lazenby? I wonder how he'll control it. As for tomorrow, we're probably all dead by morning if we –' and here he looks at you and Amy, 'don't sort this out soon.'

To meet Lazenby to find out more about the werewolves, go to 54.

To head straight for the ruins, go to 69.

You tell the Doctor to go ahead to stop the Wolf Stone and you head out of the monastery, away from the light, but it's still illuminating everything for as far as the eye can see. You think that you must be able to see the light from hundreds of miles away, it reaches so high.

You eventually meet a squad of black-uniformed soldiers, armed to the teeth. They ask who you are and what you're doing there. You tell them as much as you can about the werewolves – which they seem to know about already – the light source, the Doctor and the Wolf Stone.

They try to walk past you but you ask them to stop.

'Get out of the way,' says the leader. 'We'll show these werewolves who's in charge here. We'll round them up and cage them. They'll be no harm to anyone.'

Suddenly you don't feel so good. 'That's just it,' you say, then pause as the burning sensation starts to return in your blood, 'if you go in there it'll be a bloodbath and the Doctor won't be able to save anyone.'

The soldier looks at you hard. 'What's wrong with you?'

If you tell him, go to 43.

If you lie and say there's nothing wrong, go to 59.

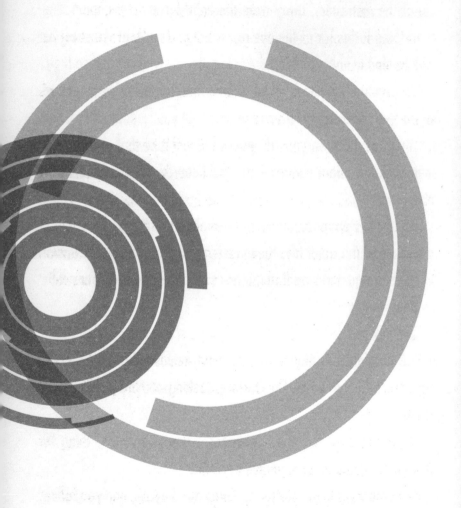

The Doctor isn't happy that you think the rest of the werewolves should be destroyed. 'The people in here, they're victims, too.'

You feel as if you should apologise — but you really are running out of time and ideas!

'We can see the people,' ruminates the Doctor. 'This stone, it's extracting the werewolf from them.'

'You mean it's fixing them?' you ask. Could it be that simple?

'I think this stone, with all this fresh earth around it, has only recently emerged. It's needed this particular path of the moon to cross this particular point. It's needed this moment and a critical mass of werewolf DNA. I think it's a gene re-sequencer. It's about to transmit a signal around the world that'll turn every human into a werewolf.'

'Whoa!'

'Yes, 'whoa!''

Every werewolf is now in mid-air, held somehow by the beams of light from the vast pillar. The Doctor is looking at a body high off the ground.

'Right, you two,' he says, 'come here. There's only one thing for it — you're going to have to give me a lift.'

He clambers onto the platform. 'Come on!' he calls, and you follow. The column of light is dazzling and you're certain it's glowing brighter.

'Stand either side of me. You're going to fire me into that beam—'

'You're mad if—' interrupts Amy, but the Doctor stops her.

'There's no time, Amy! Please! Trust me!' he implores. 'The lives of billions could be over in a moment! Trust me!'

'If you don't live to regret this, you'll be sorry!' says Amy, knitting her fingers together to act as a step for the Doctor. You do the same.

'Here goes nothing,' says the Doctor. 'As soon as I put my second foot down, throw me up.'

He puts one foot on Amy's hands and as soon as his second foot steps onto yours, you both fire him as high into the air as you can – and straight into the beam of light. The Doctor, pierced by the fierce ray, screams in pain.

'What's he doing?' you ask Amy, not taking your eyes off the Doctor. You see a swirling pattern of golden light travel from the Doctor's body.

'The Doctor's not human,' she explains. 'He's adding a bit of himself into the mix. He'd better be right, or we're about to become super-smart and super-annoying werewolves.'

The moment the golden energy strands from the Doctor reach the pillar of light, the ground quakes.

'Cross your fingers!' says Amy.

The stone makes a cracking noise and you and Amy leap down. The beams shut off, and everyone falls to the floor. You race to the Doctor lying on the ground. 'Can we not do that again in a hurry, please?

I ache everywhere.'

The column of light flickers madly, creating a strobe effect before abruptly going out. The platform suddenly shatters with a massive 'crumpf!' – and, best of all, you're still human! The Doctor did it!

'The transmitter needed haemovariform DNA information to send around the world. I just put my Time Lord biology in the way.'

'Won't that make everyone a little bit Time Lord?' asks Amy.

'Not at all – the machine didn't know what to do with me and simply shut down. I've never been an off-switch before.'

'You weren't sure it'd work, were you?' you ask.

The Doctor smiles down at you, his face lit only by the moon. 'Something had to be done, didn't it? And what are we going to do with all these people?'

You look around the room – even moonlight is revealing too much. There are dozens of people around you, stark naked!

'I think this lot can sort out their own clothing problems,' says the Doctor. 'And it's time we got you home, isn't it? Don't you have school in the morning? Come on!'

THE END

The Doctor looks at you critically. 'We could smash it to pieces, but mindless violence never really solved anything, did it?'

Amy adds, 'Don't mind the Doctor. He can be very rude.'

'I am trying to save the world here,' says the Doctor. 'Again. That's twice this week at the very least!' And he goes back to investigating the Wolf Stone.

'Smashing the Stone might also leave an awful lot of hungry werewolves behind,' says Amy gently. 'And we'd probably be dinner.'

To try to investigate the Wolf Stone some more, go to 58.

To investigate the room further, go to 72.

'And how do you suggest that I stop the moon?' asks the Doctor, waving his hands in the air as if that's the most stupid thing he's ever heard in his life. 'Shall I just grow 385,000 kilometres tall and knock it out of its orbit? Or should I find a very long stick? What about if… I…' He stops, pauses, turns back to you and says, 'Hold on, though! It's not the moon that's the problem, is it?'

'It isn't?' say you and Amy together.

'No, it's not the moon, it's the moonlight! It's this particular wavelength of light that's powering this machinery. All we have to do is stop the light!'

Then he starts fiddling with his sonic screwdriver and you hear him mutter something about 'refractive index', then he starts rushing around all the people being held in mid-air by the alien machine.

'Check that everyone has become human! Quickly!'

All three of you race around, half in panic, half in excitement. The Doctor hasn't told you his plan but you know he's got something up his sleeve! Within a couple of minutes you've checked everyone and the three of you are standing by the last beam of light showing any signs of the strange purple strands – haemovariform DNA – that the machine has extracted from the werewolves.

'Right, either this works or we're all done for. It's been nice knowing you both.' With that, the Doctor raises his sonic screwdriver as high as he can and the air ripples around you. You look up – the moon has vanished!

'How did you do that?!'

You look around in astonishment and then notice that you can't see the edges of the room, or further into the fields around the monastery, but you can see where the column of light ends – and that's only metres above the Doctor's head.

'I've changed the refractive index of the air about twenty or so metres above us,' he explains. 'No light can get in. With no moonlight, this piece of alien madness,' he says, kicking the strange stone, 'should just stop!'

As if on cue, the beams from the central column cut out, causing a few dozen bodies to tumble to the ground. No one, as far as you can tell, seems to be hurt – and everyone of them is naked!

Suddenly, a huge cloud of black smoke erupts from the stone.

'Cor! What a stink!' cries the Doctor, as the column of light goes out. In utter darkness, you feel the ground shaking beneath your feet. You can't see your hands in front of your face. Everything is completely black until the stone starts sparking and you can just make out the Doctor with his arm held high.

'Doctor!' cries Amy. 'Get down from there! That thing's going to blow up!'

With an almighty 'crumpf!' the stone explodes into a million pieces – but did the Doctor get away? You can't see a thing as bits of the stone platform rain down.

Brushing small fragments from your hair, you realise you can see the moon again. Your eyes adjust to the gloom – and there's the Doctor!

'Come on, you two – let's get to the TARDIS and let this lot here at the wardrobe. I don't think I'll have ever seen the ship so full. And then it's time to take you home, isn't it?'

You nod your head, sad that your time with the Doctor is over.

'But,' he adds, 'I think you deserve to take the scenic route!'

THE END

EMPIRE OF THE WOLF

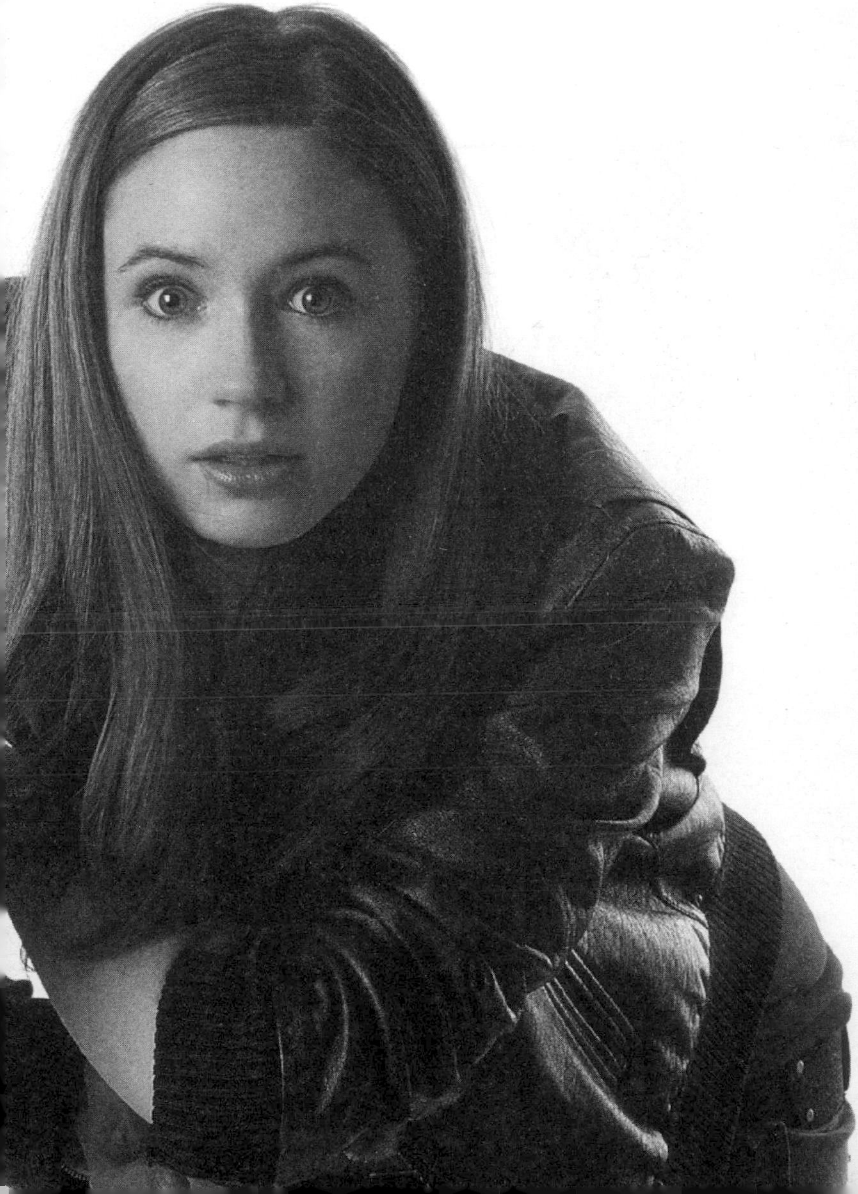

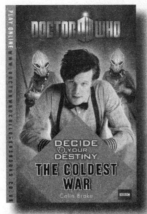